FOR LOVE OF LIBERTY
A Silver Lining Ranch Series Prequel

Published by Julie Lessman, LLC
Copyright © 2017 by Julie Lessman

ASIN: B071K6ZQJH

Cover Design and Interior Format

For

LOVE

of

LIBERTY

SILVER LINING RANCH SERIES

PREQUEL NOVEL

JULIE LESSMAN

ACCLAIM FOR JULIE LESSMAN

"Truly masterful plot twists ..."
—Romantic Times Book Reviews

"Readers who like heartwarming novels, such as those written by Debbie Macomber, are sure to enjoy this book."
—Booklist Online

"Julie is one of the best there is today at writing intensely passionate romance novels. Her ability to thread romance and longing, deception and forgiveness, and lots of humor are unparalleled by anyone else in the Christian market today."
—Rachel McRae of *LifeWay Stores*

"Julie Lessman's prose and character development is masterful."
—Church Libraries Magazine

AUTHOR ACCLAIM FOR
JULIE LESSMAN

"In Isle of Hope Lessman tells a poignant tale of first loves reunited and families reconciled. Both emotionally captivating and spiritually challenging, this sweet southern love story deals with issues of forgiveness and restoration. Fans of Lessman will be absolutely delighted with this riveting tale!" —Denise Hunter, bestselling author of Falling Like Snowflakes

"In Isle of Hope, award-winning author Julie Lessman weaves a story of how past choices collide with future consequences. Lessman's novel has it all: lush details, dynamic characters, and a storyline that keeps you turning the pages. The characters Lessman created in Isle of Hope confront their (in)ability to forgive – and as you fall in love with these characters, be prepared to question your beliefs about forgiveness." —Beth K. Vogt, author of Crazy Little Thing Called Love, and a 2015 RITA® Finalist and a 2015 and 2014 Carol Award finalist

"Fans of Julie Lessman's historical romances will love this modern day love story! Isle of Hope is a heartwarming and inspirational novel about forgiveness sought and restoration found. I'm enamored with the large and wonderful O'Bryen family and I thoroughly enjoyed the romances Julie skillfully crafted for both Jack O'Bryen and his mom Tess. A delight!" —Becky Wade, award-winning author of My Stubborn Heart and The Porter Family series including A Love Like Ours

"Truly masterful plot twists ..." —Romantic Times Book Reviews

"Readers who like heartwarming novels, such as those written by Debbie Macomber, are sure to enjoy this book." —Booklist Online

"Julie is one of the best there is today at writing intensely passionate romance novels. Her ability to thread romance and longing, deception and forgiveness, and lots of humor are unparalleled by anyone else in the Christian market today." —Rachel McRae of LifeWay Stores

"Julie Lessman's prose and character development is masterful." —Church Libraries Magazine

"With memorable characters and an effervescent plot that's as buoyant as it is entertaining, Dare to Love Again is Julie Lessman at her zestful best." —Tamera Alexander, bestselling author of A Lasting Impression and To Whisper Her Name

"In a powerful and skillfully written novel, Lessman exposes raw human emotions, proving once again that it's through our greatest pain that God can lead us to our true heart, revealed and restored. Thoroughly enthralling!" — Maggie Brendan, author of the Heart of the West and The Blue Willow Brides series

"Julie Lessman brings all her passion for romance rooted in her passion for God to A Heart Revealed. Emma Malloy is her finest heroine yet. These characters, with their own personal struggles and the ignited flame of an impossible love, fill the pages of this powerful, passionate, fast-paced romance." —Mary Connealy, bestselling author of the Lassoed in Texas, Montana Marriages, Trouble in Texas, and Wild at Heart series

"What an interesting mix of characters. Rather than a single boy-meets-girl romance, Julie Lessman's latest novel takes readers on an emotional roller coaster with several couples—some married, some yearning to be married—as they seek to embrace love, honor the Lord, and uncover a dark truth that's been hidden for a decade. Readers who long for passion in their love stories will find it in abundance here!" —Liz Curtis Higgs, bestselling author of Thorn in My Heart

"Readers will not be able to part with these characters come 'The End." —Laura Frantz, award-winning author of Love's Reckoning

"With an artist's brushstroke, Julie Lessman creates another masterpiece filled with family and love and passion. Love at Any Cost will not only soothe your soul, but it will make you laugh, stir your heart, and release a sigh of satisfaction when you turn the last page." —MaryLu Tyndall, bestselling author of Veil of Pearls

CHARACTERS

THE HERO:
Griffin Alexander McShane: Director of the V&T Railroad in Virginia City, Nevada and the heroine's childhood nemesis.

THE HEROINE:
Liberty (Libby) Margaret O'Shea: Newly graduated from Vassar, suffragette, and journalist at the Territorial Enterprise newspaper in Virginia City.

THE REST OF THE CAST:
Milo Parks: Finn McShane's best friend.

Pastor Poppy: Minister who took Finn under his wing after Finn's father deserted the family.

Mrs. Poppy: Pastor Poppy's wife, town matriarch, and matchmaker.

Maeve O'Shea: Liberty's mother.

Aiden O'Shea: Liberty's father and banker in Virginia City.

Kitty Faye Jones: Liberty's best friend.

Martha Artyomenko: Liberty's other best friend.

Jo Beth Templeton: The girl Finn is seeing and daughter of banker George Templeton.

Miss (Wilhelmina) Willoughby: Finn's & Liberty's teacher in school.

Bettie Boswell: Jo Beth's best friend.

Gertie: The O'Shea's cook and maid.

DEDICATION

To Marlene Dickerson, Julie Graves, Wendi
Kitsteiner, Bonnie Roof, Virginia Rush, Sherida
Stewart, and Kate Voss—whose kind hearts and
keen eyes (on this book or others) have blessed
me more than I can say. Thank you
for your precious friendships!

It is for liberty that Christ has set us free.
—Galatians 5:1

PROLOGUE

Virginia City, 1860

" **A**BOMINABLE."
Miss Willoughby's voice rang clear and concise
from the back of the schoolroom, spelling primer in hand
as she offered fourteen-year-old Liberty "Libby" O'Shea
an encouraging smile. "Since everyone has been eliminated
from the spelling bee except you and Mr. McShane, Miss
O'Shea, we'll need both the definition and usage of the
word in a sentence in addition to the spelling, all right?"

"Yes, ma'am." Libby's smile tightened, the presence of
seventeen-year-old Griffin McShane a few feet away gird-
ing her with the resolve to put the cocky know-it-all in
his place. "Abominable," she repeated in a loud voice, her
mind immediately tracking to the most appropriate definition: *Griffin McVain.*

She cleared her throat. "A-b-o-m-i-n-a-b-l-e. Definition: something unpleasant, disagreeable, repulsive,
disgusting, loathsome, nauseating, insufferable, despicable,
and horrible. Sentence usage ..." She bit back the squirm
of a smile. *Griffin McShane is an abominable rogue.* Shoulders
square, she notched her chin up. "Spilling ink on a class-
mate's term paper is an abominable thing to do."

Snickers filtered throughout the room, and Libby hoped

he was as embarrassed as she always was when he taunted her, but she doubted it. He seemed to thrive on attention, good or bad, *and* trying to upstage Libby whenever he could. Ever since she'd moved here from New York a year ago, he'd been the proverbial thorn in her side—taunting her, pranking her, *challenging her.*

Back in New York, she'd always been the top student with little or no effort, the teacher's favorite and a shining star in every school she'd ever attended. *Until* her father was transferred to Virginia City to open a bank on the heels of the gold rush and the subsequent Comstock Lode, the first major silver discovery in the United States. Overnight, Libby found herself playing second fiddle to the most obnoxious boy in town, dirt poor in both wealth and manners.

But filthy rich in pride.

And, unfortunately, good looks, which only riled Libby all the more.

"Correct," Miss Willoughby said with approval, the twinkle in her eyes the only indication she understood the pointed meaning of Libby's sentence. With a perfunctory clear of her throat, the teacher averted her attention to the "abominable" class rake who excelled in everything from academics to emotional harassment. "Mr. McShane, your word is 'irascibility.'"

"Irascibility." The baritone voice that always carried a hint of a smile rang through the classroom with that same annoying confidence that managed to charm the socks off every female within a 5-mile radius. Whether teacher, parent, or child, it didn't matter. If Griffin McShane smiled at them, there seemed to be a collective sigh of approval, especially from the teen-aged girls in town. Libby's lids narrowed as she chanced a peek out of the corner of her eye.

All except the smart ones …

"I-r-a-s-c-i-b-i-l-i-t-y," he said with a leisurely slack of his hip, thumbs nonchalantly tucked into the faded suspenders of patched and dusty trousers. His manner was casual, almost like he was chewing the fat with friends rather than competing for the honor of Virginia City's scholar of the year. "Definition: behavior that is short-tempered, testy, touchy, petulant, waspish, prickly, or snippy."

Libby's lips compressed as she studied his sculpted face shadowed with stubble way too pronounced for seventeen years. His carefree manner never failed to unnerve her, as if everything came so easily for him—the grades, the athletic skills, the popularity. It just wasn't fair, especially since the only effort he seemed to put forth was in goading her. Easily one of the tallest boys in town, he filled out the worn linsey-woolsey shirt with a brawn that defied his age, honed from afternoons working at the lumber mill, no doubt. Which irked Libby all the more since she attended school full-time to his mere mornings, yet *still* struggled to best him in class.

"Sentence usage," he continued with that trademark trace of tease, "The mare's irascibility confirmed that what she lacked in patience, she made up for in temper."

Titters circled the class as Libby's cheeks bloomed bright red, well aware that Griffin *McPain* intended to win the war of words as well as the spelling bee.

Miss Willoughby's smile crooked. "Correct, Mr. McShane, although I'm sure the mare would disagree." Her gaze flicked back to Libby, the encouraging sparkle in her eyes lending support. "Miss O'Shea, your word is supersede."

Adrenaline pulsed through Libby's veins, the thrill of victory surging along with it. "Supersede," she said with certainty, "s-u-p-e-r-c-e-d-e. Definition: replace, take the place of, succeed, supplant, displace, oust, overthrow, remove, or unseat." *Like I am going to do to you, Mr. McShame.* "Sentence usage: The brightest and best will always supersede those who think they are." Unable to resist a satisfied glance in McShane's direction, Libby returned her attention to Miss Willoughby.

Right before her body went stone cold.

The sympathetic crimp of Miss Willoughby's brows confirmed Libby's greatest fear. "I'm sorry, Miss O'Shea, but your spelling is incorrect," the teacher said with a compassionate smile before she turned her attention to Griffin. "Mr. McShane, please spell supersede."

"With pleasure, Miss Willoughby," Griffin's answer came, the air of self-assurance in his voice infusing Libby's pale cheeks with an embarrassing whoosh of heat. "Supersede. S-u-p-e-r-s-e-d-e."

Silence hung thick in the air as Libby's lungs refused to work, stomach contracting at the slow nod of Miss Willoughby's head. "Absolutely correct, Mr. McShane. It's been a tight race between you and Miss O'Shea, but you have emerged as Virginia City's Scholar of the Year, young man, so congratulations!"

"Yay, Griff!" his buddies shouted around the room, vaulting up with whoops and hollers while his best friend, Milo Parks, hoisted him in the air, the two of them carrying on like they were eight instead of almost eighteen.

Libby's best friends, Kitty Jones and Martha Artyomenko, surrounded her with sympathetic hugs that matched the kind understanding in Miss Willoughby's eyes. "Excellent job as well, Miss O'Shea," her teacher said with a soft smile, "and there's always next year, young lady."

Yes, next year. Libby offered her teacher a grateful smile. When Griffin *McBlame* would be graduated and long gone. Her frustration drifted out on a gentle sigh of resignation as she squeezed her best friends' hands. Perhaps it was just as well that he won Scholar of the Year. After all, as the sole support of his mother and younger siblings, she supposed he needed all the success he could get, no matter how awful he was to her.

Gulping in a deep draw of air, she turned to offer him a stiff handshake, her smile bright if somewhat forced.

"Congratulations, Griffin. You are a formidable foe."

His hand swallowed hers, and it galled her to no end that her stomach fluttered when he gave her that slow, easy grin. "Why, thank you, Liberty Bell," he said, drawling out that annoying nickname he always used just to get on her nerves. "I may have gotten the spelling right, but don't forget that you got a lot right too."

She blinked, not used to compliments from her nemesis.

"Why … thank you, Griffin," she said with a wide expanse of eyes, cheeks heating when his firm grasp lingered, his smile as warm as the hand holding hers.

"You bet." His thumb gently grazed the top of her wrist, sending shivers all the way up her arm. "After all, Miss Bell," he said in a soft voice that belied the twinkle in his eye, "you're right on the mark more than you know, especially today." Flashing his trademark smile, he turned and strolled away, tossing the final word over his shoulder along with a saucy wink. "'The brightest and best *will* always supersede those who think they are.'"

CHAPTER ONE

Virginia City, Nevada, May 1868

O KAY, JUST BREATHE ... IN, out, in, out. Twenty-two-year-old Liberty O'Shea swallowed hard, her throat as dry as the clouds of dust whirling behind her from wagon wheels on F Street at noon. Sucking in a shallow breath ripe with the smell of horse manure and tobacco, she gripped the brass doorknob of the Virginia & Truckee Railroad office, knuckles pinched whiter than the lacey gloves on her hand. "I can do this," she whispered.

If I don't throw up first.

Shoulders back, she pushed the door open, determined to conquer the task at hand—a newspaper interview with the V&T director about a 21-mile railroad line from Virginia City to Carson City. An interview that could very well secure a spot on one of Virginia City's most prestigious newspapers where Mark Twain himself was once an editor—the *Territorial Enterprise.* Libby reminded herself to exhale. Or at least that's what Milo Parks had promised when he'd given her this trial assignment. Her mouth veered sideways as she quietly closed the door. *That is, if* one can trust a boy who'd once bolted her in the school outhouse.

With a skunk.

"Can I help you, miss?" A young woman glanced up

from a battered oak desk, her faded maroon silk dress so tight, she could have been waiting tables at the Brass Rail Saloon. In reflex, Libby glanced down at her own expensive House of Worth walking suit. Its butternut silk was the perfect complement to her flaming auburn hair, which now peeked out beneath the latest feathered straw hat from Paris. For one brief moment, she felt horribly extravagant next to this poor working woman attired in no more than a shabby barroom dress. Summoning a smile, she quickly shook it off, reminding herself that in a man's world, she needed to be at her very best in order to further the cause of women everywhere, including the poor soul before her.

"Yes, thank you." Libby hugged a pad of paper to her ruffled white bodice, gaze flicking to the wood-slatted wall behind the young woman, its knotted pine emblazoned with a map of Nevada. Her lips instinctively pursed over the dotted line that connected Virginia City with Carson City, reminding her of her disdain for railroads. Tucking her reticule behind the pad, she worked hard to convey her most confident smile. "Mr. Milo Parks suggested I interview Director Finn for a feature article in the *Territorial Enterprise*. Is he in?"

A ghost of a smile flickered across the woman's rouged lips as she shuffled papers into a neat stack and laid them aside. "Yes, Director Finn is in today, but I'm afraid he just stepped out for lunch and a few errands, so I'm not exactly sure when he'll be back."

Disappointment dampened Libby's spirits as she chewed on the edge of her lip. *Rats!* As a spanking new graduate of Vassar for all of one week, she had hoped to cinch the newspaper position—today, if possible—in order to embark upon her true calling: women's rights in her home state of Nevada. Her mouth cemented with the same determination that had won her valedictorian of her class. A 'calling' that drew her to the women's suffrage movement like miners to gold. Or in Nevada's case—silver.

Her eyes flitted to a rail clock mounted on the far wall that registered just past eleven, and her limbs stiffened along with her spine. Well, if the director didn't take the whole livelong day, she could possibly complete the interview and write the article before Milo left. Spirits climbing, she offered another smile. "Would it be all right if I waited for him in his office?" she asked, noting the absence of chairs in the small reception area.

"Suit yourself." The young woman rose and led her to a bubbled glass door, holding it open while Libby sailed through into an office that was remarkably neat. Noting the impressive stack of paperwork on the polished cherry-wood desk—perfectly staggered in a precise row off to the side—Libby settled into the matching cordovan leather chair.

The woman at the door gave a short cough, the sound almost tinged with a smile. "Uh, who should I tell the director is waiting to see him?"

"Liberty Margaret O'Shea," Libby said with no little pride, "on assignment for the *Territorial Enterprise,* if you please." *And from God,* she thought with a sudden rush of excitement. *To help provide justice for all, whether in race or gender.* "Thank you, Miss—"

The half smile was back. "Delilah. You want a cup of swill?"

Libby blinked. "'Swill'?"

"Director Finn likes his coffee as thick as the sludge they use on their blasted steam engines, so there ain't no other word for it. But you're welcome to it if you want."

"Uh ... no, but thank you, Miss Delilah." Libby smiled as she took a seat, grateful when the woman partially closed the door, leaving it ajar. Laying her pad and purse on the edge of the desk, she scanned the cozy office, breathing in the pleasant scent of leather, lime, and—she closed her eyes, trying to place the wonderful smell that lingered in the room—*mint?* Her nose automatically wrinkled, the scent conjuring up memories that were anything but pleasant. *Of one Griffin Alexander McShane.*

Against her will, a shiver whispered down her spine, and she shook it off, jumping up to roam the office instead. Never had she been more grateful than now that her former archenemy had gone to work for the Central Pacific Railroad after graduation, taking him far away from Virginia City to Sacramento. *Although* Libby had her doubts that either the Sierra Nevada mountain range *or* the West Coast was far enough away to suit her. Not after he'd broken her heart her senior year, proving he was every bit the fortune hunter her father had proclaimed him to be. A hint of a smile shadowed her lips, helping to chase the awful memory away. But at least she'd won Scholar of the Year the next four years after he graduated, something that not only honed her desire to excel in college, but in everything she put her hand to.

Especially securing a woman's right to vote in Nevada.

Absently perusing the office, she studied a beautiful photograph of the same Sierra Nevada Mountains that presided over Virginia City and her family's own Ponderosa Pines Ranch. Her focus suddenly sharpened as she realized every wall in the room was graced with various framed photographs of Nevada scenery, each more magnificent than the last. "Oh my goodness." Her hand fluttered to her chest as she gave the pictures her full attention, mesmerized by the raw beauty before her. "These are absolutely stupendous," she said out loud, in awe of anyone who possessed such talent for capturing the true spirit of her home state.

"Why, thank you, Miss O'Shea," a deep voice said behind her, humor clearly lacing its tone. "I do believe that's the first genuine compliment you may have ever given me. Unless, of course, you meant 'stupid' instead of 'stupendous.'"

Libby whirled around so fast, her straw hat went askew, fluttering its feathers and dislodging a wisp of auburn hair that dangled over her eye. Her body flashed hot and then cold, stomach plunging to the toes of her kid leather boots along with the blood from her cheeks.

Nope, "stupid" was definitely the right word. She gulped.

For me.

CHAPTER TWO

"**M**R. MC ... *MCVAIN* ... w-what are you d-doing here?" Liberty rasped, fire blasting her cheeks over the slip of her own personal nickname for the pest from her past. Her question came out more of a croak as she attempted to secure her hat with pins that quivered as much as her stomach.

One thick, dark brow jagged high as a smile played on his full lips. "McVain?"

More blood surged into her face, so hot that her hands broke out in a sweat along with her brow. "I ... I m-mean, Mr. McShane. Are you here to see Director Finn too?"

That languid smile went to work as he strolled in. He bypassed her altogether to take the seat behind the desk with a twinkle in light brown eyes a shade lighter than her suit. "No, ma'am, I'm afraid I *am* Director Finn."

She stared, barely able to string two coherent thoughts together. "I ... I d-don't understand. Instead of McShane?"

"Nope." Gaze fused to hers, he slowly removed an impeccable sack suit jacket and draped it over his chair before taking his seat, rolling the sleeves of his pinstripe shirt to reveal corded forearms matted with hair. A faint smile hovered on his handsome face while he loosened his string tie and the top two buttons of a silk waistcoat, his relaxed manner in total contrast to her own paralysis. Mouth twitching, he lounged back in his chair with hands propped behind his neck. "Instead of Griffin."

All she could do was blink.

A mischievous flash of white teeth took her years back to toads in her lunch pail and worms in her inkwell. He ducked his head in tease, tumbling several dark curls over his forehead while those hazel eyes sparkled with mischief. "As in Grif-*fin?*" His sculpted nose wrinkled in jest. "Not sure that fancy college helped all that much, Libs—you seemed a whole lot smarter back in high school."

Fire scalded her face, igniting her temper. "Wish I could say the same for you, *Mr. Finn.*"

His husky laughter ricocheted off the walls as he plopped long legs on his desk, pressed charcoal trousers somehow at odds with leather boots in dire need of a polish.

Like their owner.

"Now *that's* what I was shooting for," he quipped with that maddening twinkle in his eyes, "a little sound and fury from my Liberty Bell."

Libby slapped two hands on her hips and stepped forward. "For your information, Mr. *McVain*, I am not *your* Liberty Bell, and I'll thank you to stop calling me that."

The grin eased into a crooked smile as he idly scratched the back of his neck. "I don't know, Miss Bell. You're cold as steel and make an awful lot of noise, so if the bell rings …"

She stamped her foot, feeling all of fourteen again. "The only 'ringing' going on here, Mr. *McShane*, will be around your neck if you continue this juvenile behavior." Snatching her notebook and reticule from the edge of the desk, she hugged both to her chest, chin in a jut. "When will Superintendent Yerington be in the office?"

"Well, let's see now …" He glanced at his pocket watch, then peered up with a hint of humor in eyes that may have softened a hair. His brows tented with a touch of sympathy. "His office is actually in Carson City, so … Fourth of July?" He sighed and dropped his feet to the floor with a thud, hands resting on the arms of his chair as he studied her intently. "Looks like you're stuck with me, Miss O'Shea, since I am the one and only representative for the Virginia & Truckee Railroad in all of Virginia City."

Libby's jaw dropped a full inch. *Blue blistering blazes!* She bit her tongue, gripping her pad and reticule so hard, her fingers were now as bloodless as her face. "I'll just have to take the stage to Carson City, then."

He peeked at his watch again and grimaced. "*Wellllll,* the next stage doesn't leave till tomorrow morning, and over and above the four hours you'd have to travel one way—barring any holdups or Indian raids, of course—I'm afraid Superintendent Yerington is back East for his sister's wedding."

Dirty drawers of the Devil! All hope seeped out along with the air in Libby's lungs, sagging both her shoulders and her morale.

He rose and extended a remarkably calloused hand for a man in a suit, his voice suddenly gentle as he nodded toward the chair beside her. "Look, Liberty, have a seat, please, and let's start over, shall we? I think it's time we both put the past behind, don't you?"

She assessed the sincerity of the man before her, who now offered a handshake over his desk, and wondered if she could trust him. Whenever she'd tried in the past, she'd found herself locked in an outhouse or washing ink out of her hair.

Or a laughingstock when he'd jilted her for Jo Beth.

Still, those light brown eyes were suddenly as rich and warm as Papa's Best Irish whiskey—almost amber in the light that streamed through his side window. And, no doubt, just as capable of making her dizzy. Like the summer of her senior year when they'd actually gotten along as festival volunteers for a brief period of time.

Till he broke my heart …

She sucked in a deep draw of air, and the scent of Bay Rum and peppermint flooded her senses. Her gaze flicked to his hand and back while those caramel-colored eyes locked on hers with a depth and honesty she'd never seen in him before. Expelling a silent breath, she slowly reached out, emitting a tiny squeak at a spark of static electricity when his hand swallowed hers.

Grip firm, he offered a smile that warmed her more than the lock of his palm. "Hello, my name is Griffin Alexander McShane, but my friends call me Finn, a nickname coined by my niece at the age of two, who had trouble pronouncing 'G's.'"

As natural as breathing, her lips tipped into a smile. "And my name is Liberty Margaret O'Shea, and all I can say is the saints preserve us if the niece is half the scamp as her uncle."

He grinned, and two dangerously deep dimples winked, imparting a woozy sensation in the pit of her stomach. "'Scamp?'" His low laughter filled the small room, surrounding her like a hug, husky and warm. "I think the words you may be looking for are scoundrel and scalawag, Miss O'Shea, which brings me to a long-overdue apology for being less than chivalrous in school." He released her hand with a wink that weakened the tendons at the back of her knees, conveniently, if not gracelessly, plopping her into the chair.

Still standing, he leaned forward with a brace of palms to the desk and a smile that dazzled as much as the boyish twinkle in his eyes. "So ... am I forgiven?"

CHAPTER THREE

*F*ORGIVEN? LIBERTY GULPED. *AND THEN some.* "I suppose that depends on the interview, Mr. McShane," she said, her voice a little too breathless to suit.

"Call me Finn, please, Miss O'Shea." The dimples made an encore appearance, all but guaranteeing consent to anything he asked. "Unless, of course, you allow me the 'liberty' to use your Christian name?"

She strove for casual despite the white-knuckled choke-hold she had on the purse and pad in her lap. "Certainly, Finn. As long as there's no bell attached, we should be golden." Releasing a shallow breath of air, she willed her body to relax, taking a stab at humor. "Or maybe that should be silver, given the wealth of mines tunneling through our hills."

"Exactly," he said, his demeanor suddenly more serious as he settled back in his chair with a loose fold of arms. "Which neatly brings us back to your original purpose, I believe—an interview about the proposed railroad?"

Just the sound of the word "interview" pumped adrenalin into Libby's veins. She retrieved a pencil from her purse and placed the pad of paper on top, ready to record the truth of what the V&T Railroad had in mind for the welfare of their laborers. "So, Finn, can you tell me a bit about the ambitions of the Virginia & Truckee Railroad?"

His pause was barely noticeable, so smooth was his pre-sentation, elbows now propped on the arms of his chair while he watched her over the clasp of his hands. "Certainly, Liberty. The V&T Railroad Company was incorporated in March of this year to serve the mines of the Comstock. As you are no doubt aware, a railroad was deemed necessary due to the exorbitant cost of freighting goods by wagon, as well as the transport of ore to the mills along the Carson River."

"Of course," Libby said with a solemn nod, well aware a railroad would be a huge boon to Virginia City, even if her father's bank hadn't won the business.

"We hope to break ground next February, with grading crews beginning two miles below Gold Hill on American Flats. Completion is slated for the end of the year."

Libby's ears instantly perked at the mention of grading crews, and scooting to the edge of her chair, she fixed him with a penetrating stare, pencil poised over her paper. "You mention crews. Can you tell me what provisions are being made for the safety and care of the men you employ?"

His eyelids narrowed almost imperceptibly, barely noticeable with the polite smile that stole over his chiseled features. "The V&T Railroad Company is committed to the safety and well-being of its workers, Liberty, I can assure you of that."

"And fair pay, Finn? Is V&T committed to that as well, or do they plan to follow in the footsteps of the Central Pacific Railroad? Where, as you know, Chinese workers were paid a dollar a day without room and board while the Irish workers"—she inclined her head to underscore her point—"such as yourself, were paid two dollars per day, *plus* room and board."

Despite his calm demeanor, Libby saw a storm brewing in eyes that seemed to darken along with his mood. "The V&T Railroad Company is *not* Central Pacific, Miss O'Shea. As one of the shortest independent lines in the world, we have a vested interest in Nevada. We are Nevadans, just like you, whether Chinese or white, and our pay scale will reflect that with honesty and integrity, unlike Central Pacific."

"And yet I was told you were in Central Pacific's employ, rising through the ranks while crews were worked from sunrise to sunset, six days a week, were you not, Mr. McShane?" Her temper thinned along with his eyes, their gazes going head-to-head. "Can you assure me it won't be the same for the crews of Virginia & Truckee?"

He leaned in, the tic in his cheek keeping time with the throb of her pulse. "I can assure a solid wage for a solid day's work, Miss O'Shea, for any man willing to give his all during a fairly short but very lucrative period of time."

She jutted a brow. "His 'all,' Mr. McShane? Or his life? I've read about corpses of Chinese laborers found in the spring after horrendous snowstorms during tunnel construction, frozen solid like marble, tools still in their hands."

She noted a dangerous shift in his jaw but didn't care, too incensed over the vile racial inequalities in which the high-and-mighty railroads indulged. "Tell me, Mr. McShane, can you ensure Chinese laborers won't be forced to sacrifice their lives on the altar of greed and the almighty deadline?"

"Even the almighty railroads cannot control the weather, Miss O'Shea," he ground out, teeth milled tight.

Her blood began to boil. "No, but safety precautions can be put in place, sir, can they not? To help protect the very workers who are putting money in *your* pocket?" She leaned in like he had, the tension between them sparking more than the static electricity from the handshake they'd shared. "Will you assure me weather safety provisions will be implemented even though Central Pacific failed to do so when you were on their payroll?"

He shot to his feet, palms knuckle-white on his desk as he bent forward with fire in his eyes. "I can assure you, Miss Bell, that I will do everything in my power to safeguard our crews, including the implementation of safety measures that CP failed to do. And for your information, ma'am, the management at Central Pacific and I did not see eye to eye on a number of points, which is why I took my leave to work with V&T."

Oh.

She slowly sat back in her chair while he did the same, somewhat taken aback he wasn't the money-grubbing company man she'd assumed him to be. She swallowed some of the fury in her throat, a fury that always rose like bile over the injustices men inflicted upon those they deemed inferior. Like women. Avoiding his piercing gaze, she promptly wrote his response on her notepad. Even so, he had been a company man during some of the most outrageous atrocities perpetrated against Chinese laborers during the construction of the transcontinental railroad. "Well," she said with a less pointed heft of her chin, "I'm certainly glad to hear that, Mr. McShane—that possibly comforts me somewhat."

"Possibly?" He stared, mouth hanging open. "Somewhat?" He suddenly laughed and shook his head, steepling his fingers. "You know what, Libs? You're all grown up now, and yet college hasn't changed you much at all. You're still that prickly little girl I could never seem to please, so I just gave up and teased you instead." His smile was stiff.

"Well, don't be offended, please, but your 'comfort' level is not all that high on my priority list, Miss Bell."

"Really." She studied him with a calculating squint while she tapped the pencil against her chin. "Well, how about the comfort level of the people of Virginia City, Mr. McShane?" She arched a brow, her sweet tone unable to mask the threat of her words. "Where are they on your so-called priority list?"

"For the love of sanity," he muttered, the words coming on the heels of a low chuckle as he pinched the bridge of his nose. "What do you want from me, Libby—blood?"

"I want assurances, Director McShane, as do the people of Virginia City, that as a representative of Virginia and

Truckee Railroad, the lives of our Chinese residents will be protected at all costs."

A loud sigh parted from his lips as he stared at her, a trace of resignation in the crook of his half smile. "All right, Miss O'Shea, you have my complete assurance."

"I have your word on that?" she emphasized with a duck of her head, gaze pinned to his. "That as Director of the Virginia & Truckee Railroad, you and your railroad will take every precaution to eliminate fatalities, be they from weather, poor working conditions, or blasting?"

His smile faded. "I am not God, Miss O'Shea, no matter how exalted your opinion of me may be. I can certainly promise I will do everything in my power to safeguard the lives of my men, but I'm afraid nitroglycerin is not as compliant."

"Then don't use it," she said with a sudden plea in her tone, the challenge in her eyes daring him to break with the ranks of greed. "Use gunpowder instead, like they used to, before nitroglycerin murdered hundreds of Chinese workers."

He bent forward, voice clipped and low. "They-were-accidents, Miss O'Shea, not-murders, and you have no idea how many casualties there were."

"No, because Central Pacific didn't bother to keep records of"— she sat up straight on the brink of her chair, fingers gripped to the edge of his desk—"and I quote—'coolie casualties.'"

His jaw hardened as a nerve flickered in his temple. "The Chinese weren't the only casualties in the building of the railroad, Miss O'Shea—"

"No, only the majority of them ..." She eased back in the chair, her eyes never leaving his. "And the most violated."

He slammed a fist to his desk, his voice rising several octaves. "They were well-compensated, blast you, and fully aware of the risk."

"Tell that to their starving widows and babies!" she hollered back, both of them on their feet now, faces flushed and tempers high. They glared at each other for several seconds before her body cooled along with her tone, shoulders squared. "Promise there will be no nitroglycerin," she whispered, purse and pad to her chest.

He loomed with palms propped, eyes all but cauterizing her to the spot as he bit out every single word. "The only thing I'll promise is that no pampered, upper-crust daddy's girl with more feathers in her head than her hat is going to march in here—"

She bludgeoned a lacy glove to his desk. "Promise or I will launch a campaign to make you comply, and *I-will-win!*"

Slowly rising to his full height, he stared, arms slack at his sides while his jaw dropped in disbelief. "This never was about an interview, was it, Libby? This is about you winning—over me, over the railroad—isn't it?"

"I want a guarantee, Mr. McShane, *now*, and I want it ironclad."

"Well you got it, Miss Bell." He jerked his jacket off his chair and slashed it on, storming around his desk. She was rendered speechless when he ripped the pad and pencil from her hand and shoved them in her purse. Pushing it at her, he dragged her to the door with a hook of her elbow, voice as tight as his hold. "I *guarantee* you one thing for dead sure, ma'am—this interview is *over*."

CHAPTER FOUR

"**H**ORSE APPLES!" HER SHOUT ECHOED through the office as she skidded to a stop, heels digging in. "Not until we finish."

"Oh, we're finished ..." He commenced hauling her to the door.

"*When. Pigs. Fly,*" she said through clenched teeth, free hand anchored to the knob while her skirt flapped like a banner in the breeze strung between him and the door.

"Or pig-headed rich girls." He tried to yank her free to no avail, her hand welded to the brass as if the two were one. Halting, he whirled around, one massive finger aimed at the door. "Leave now, or I'll show you how pigs fly."

"No," she said with an upward thrust of her chin, "not until you promise."

"Fine. You won't leave?" He hurled her arm away and strode past his saucer-eyed secretary. "Then I will." Snatching his Stetson off the rack by the door, he slapped it on with a grim smile in Miss Delilah's direction. "Del, if she doesn't leave of her own accord, you have my permission to throw her out on her feathers. I'll be back when she's gone." He opened the door.

"Oh, no you don't, mister." Launching herself forward, Liberty spurted around him, arms pasted to the jambs to block his way. "We *are* going to finish this conversation."

"*Over-my-dead-body,*" he growled, heating more than her cheeks when he rudely plucked her up by the waist and set her aside so hard, she wobbled.

"Oh—good idea!" She tripped him with her foot, biting back a smile when he flailed like a puppet before regaining his balance. "But first we're going to talk, you … you … ill-mannered mule!"

"Okay, that's it." A squeak left her lips while her body took flight, her squeal quickly lost in an unladylike grunt when he tossed her over his shoulder like a sack of feed. "And I've never met a mule with manners, Miss Bell, but if I do, I'll be sure to send him over to give you some tips. Del, I'll be back shortly." He slammed the door hard, drawing the attention of several men who issued jovial greetings as they passed, their low chuckles broiling her cheeks all the more.

"Put me down right now!" she hissed, wiggling and pummeling his back with her free hand while she clutched her purse with the other. Passing the mercantile next door, she noted the dropped jaws of several well-dressed women. Another rush of blood scorched her face, both from anger and the humiliation of hanging upside down like a bat. "Let-me-down-this-instant!" she gritted out with renewed fury, battering him all the harder. "You are acting like a complete barbarian!"

"Well, no surprise there." He stomped down the wooden sidewalk, locking her legs against his chest when she tried to kick him. "What do you expect from somebody who starves babies and women—chivalry?"

"Ha!" she shouted, banging shoulders that felt like boulders while she commenced to bashing his head with her purse. "You wouldn't know the meaning of chivalry if Daniel Webster personally defined it for you, you … you … overgrown bully!"

"No, but I sure can spell it, lady, along with royal pain in the—"

"Afternoon, Finn." A man offered a casual tip of his hat, continuing on down the boardwalk as if Finn McShane manhandling a woman were an everyday occurrence.

Libby issued a grunt along with her best efforts at a pinch given the rippled steel beneath her abductor's shirt, ignoring a group of little boys who tittered close behind. "Where are you taking me?" she shouted, then bellowed a disbelieving "ouch" when he promptly returned her pinch with one of his own, the nip of his fingers against the back of her thigh igniting far more than her temper. "Did you just *pinch me?*"

"You bet, and if I could do the same to your mouth, I would."

"Why, good afternoon, Finn, and goodness me, is that Liberty O'Shea? It's so good to see you, my dear!"

"Well, that makes one of us," Finn muttered, pausing to touch the brim of his hat in deference to Mrs. Poppy, the pastor's wife. As much a part of Virginia City as the silver mines scattered across the landscape, Mrs. Poppy was a legend as the town's matchmaker, pert near pairing as many couples as Pastor Poppy hitched. Barely a smidgen over four-foot-eleven, the seventy-five-year-old matriarch had always held a special place in Libby's heart, often slipping her one of her famous poppy-seed lemon drops after church.

"Mrs. Poppy! Yes, I arrived just yesterday," Libby called as Finn continued his rampage down the wooden walkway, picking up speed, "so I'll come see you soon, I promise."

"Good girl," the old woman returned, her full rosy cheeks a familiar complement to an off-kilter silver topknot bouncing on her head. She waved as she continued on her merry way while a wagon passed with a blinding roll of dust and a cheer for Finn.

Somehow Libby managed a boot to his knee. "Finn McShane, if you don't put me down this instant ..."

"With pleasure," he said with a growl, mauling the knob of the newspaper office before kicking the door open. The receptionist froze, along with a patron who was apparently placing an ad. "Excuse me, ladies, but I have a message for Mr. Parks—won't take a moment."

"*What-are-you-doing?*" Libby whispered harshly, thrashing all the more at the prospect of making a scene at the place she hoped to work.

Completely ignoring her, he strode down the hall and kicked another door open, instantly paralyzing Milo Parks, who gaped with a pen in his hand. "Inter-view *o-ver*, Miss O'Shea," he snapped, dumping her on Milo's desk without ceremony. He aimed a thick finger, glaring at the man who'd been—until today—his best friend. "And so help me, Parks, if you send this woman down to my office ever again, our friendship is over, got it?" Without another word, he barreled out and slammed the door, rattling both it and the windows of Milo's office.

Sliding off the front of Milo's desk as discreetly as possible, Libby bit her lip while she straightened her dress with shaky fingers, throat dry at the prospect of turning around to see the horror on her prospective employer's face.

A throaty chuckle rumbled while she repinned her hat, and whirling around, her jaw swagged low at the look of utter delight on Milo Park's face. "Well, I'll be!" the assistant editor said with a clasp of hands behind his neck, slanting back in his chair with a bona fide grin. Despite Milo's amber hair to Finn's deep chestnut and his sky-blue eyes to Finn's whiskey brown, the two had always seemed like siblings to Libby, twins really, whose carefree attitudes bonded them like brothers. Only Milo had mostly been the nice brother, rarely taunting her except when his mule-headed friend had egged him on. "Haven't seen our boy that stirred up since you fleeced him in the science fair our senior year, Libs, so good job."

Her fingers froze on the pin in her hat. "You mean … you're not mad?"

"Shoot, no," Milo said with a cross of his legs on a desk scattered with galleys. "Truth be told, he's had me a mite worried lately with all the hours he's been clockin', both for the railroad during the day and then clearing his land at night. Turned into a regular workhorse when he hired on with V&T. Cuttin' way back on socializing with me or the ladies, which doesn't set well with me or them, I can tell you that." He sighed and scratched the back of his neck, eyes narrowed in thought. "It's almost like he's lost his fire, you know? So darn worried about that dad-burned land of his and the vein of silver he found, his sparkle has sorta fizzled right out." A twinkle lit in his eyes as he gave her a wink. "Till you."

Libby blinked. "I don't understand. He's a mule of a bully with a hair-trigger temper, who just kicked me out of his office and dumped me on your desk. How is that a good thing?"

Milo chuckled. "Well actually that 'mule of a bully' is one of the most mild-mannered men I know—calm, rational, steady as a rock." He flashed a grin, the glint in his eye matching the one in his teeth. "Except around you."

His smile suddenly sobered, transforming him into the professional editor she'd begged for a job mere hours ago. "Which is a good thing because he's my best friend, Libby, and frankly I'm worried about him. He doesn't smile as much as he used to and he's too blasted complacent to suit." His lips curved into a slow smile. "So I'd like to light a fire under him, and you're just the stick of dynamite I need because nobody trips his wire like you, Liberty O'Shea, *nobody*."

Head in a tilt, she studied him through slatted eyes, almost suspicious that this was some sort of trick. "Does that mean I have the job?"

He grinned. "As long as you write one heck of an editorial that stokes the logs in that boy's stove *and* you put that impressive resumé and Vassar degree to good use stirring up circulation for the *Enterprise*."

Liberty squealed and circled Milo's desk to give him

a tight hug. "Oh, Milo, thank you sooooo much, and I promise you won't regret this."

He gave her an awkward pat on the back while a ruddy shade of red bled up the length of his neck. "Nope, with your spunk and brains, Libs, I don't think I will, not even a little." The twinkle was back in his eyes as he assessed her with a pensive cock of his head. "Now our 'mule of a bully with a hair-trigger temper'?" He grinned as he picked up his pen, pausing to give her a wink. "I'm countin' on it."

CHAPTER FIVE

"THAT WAS DIRTY DEALIN', PARKS," Finn said in a near hiss after their lady friends had excused themselves to use the necessary at Flo's Diner. Gaze narrow, he eyed his best friend over the rim of his cup, his temper steaming more than the coffee. *Make that former best friend*, he thought with a healthy swig that burned all the way down—not unlike Parks sending Liberty O'Shea to his office. A low blow that had singed his mood as black and crisp as Flo's deep-fried bacon.

Milo only laughed, Finn's scowl obviously providing no censure whatsoever. "Why?" he said with a sly smile, hoisting his cup in a mock toast. "She applied for the editorial position, and her resumé was impeccable, not to mention she always could write circles around you and me. Besides, you're always grousing I never give V&T any free publicity, so I thought this trial interview was the perfect chance." He paused, assessing Finn through laughing eyes that held a hint of a dare. "Unless, of course … you're still carrying a torch for her …?"

"Oh, your bucket's full of cow chips!" Finn's usually mild manner exploded, igniting his temper hotter than that blasted torch he *wasn't* carrying for Liberty La-di-da Bell. The dad-burned richest, prettiest, smartest, touchiest female in the entire county. And, unfortunately, the only one who skittered his pulse by just giving him the evil eye, something downright rare in a town where girls usually hung all over him, giving him *way* more than the "eye." His mouth went flat. The only "hanging" Liberty wanted to do was him from a tree, the higher the better. Problem was, all she'd ever tempted *him* to do was ... touch her, hold her, tell her she drove him plum crazy with those spitfire eyes and sassy mouth. Not to mention that keen mind and wildfire passion for life he so ached to channel.

Right into loving him.

Which is exactly why he spent every moment in school harassing the daylights out of her. He was downright vexed how she made him feel inside. Angry that he wanted her. Flat-out crazy she didn't want him back. And out and out irate that she made every other girl seem like he was settling for second best.

"Come on, Finn, you were going to run into her sooner or later, right?" Milo's grin couldn't mask the concern in his eyes. "I just hurried the process along."

Wrong. Liberty O'Shea was the last person he wanted to run into. It was bad enough she still haunted the deep, dark recesses of his soul, taunting him with a longing as cruel as the taunts he used to hurl at her. Sure, he'd known he'd run into her eventually, but he'd wanted to be prepared when he did, not broadsided by an older, more sophisticated version, browsing his office as pretty as you please.

"Besides," Milo continued with a lazy sip of his coffee, "you've been a regular drudge lately, working day and night, so I thought you could use a little excitement."

One side of Finn's lip hooked. "Yeah, well, an agitated bottle of nitroglycerin would have been kinder." Huffing out a sigh, he set his coffee down to knead both temples with the pads of his fingers. "She all but came out and called me a murderer, actually accusing me of starving women and babies."

"What?" Milo's mouth fell open in a smile of disbelief.

"Yep." Finn hunched over the table, forearms flat as he took another slow sip of his coffee. "Seems my prior connection to Central Pacific has her convinced that V&T not only plans to underpay the Chinese, but blow them up in the process and starve their families to boot."

Milo's deep laughter echoed through the chintz-curtained café where he and Milo often took lunch, earning curious glances from the patrons dining around them. "You're joshing me," he said, jaw sagging so low, it looked ready to pop its hinges despite the grin on his face. "She's always been a plucky, little thing, fighting for every lost cause under the sun. I just figured she'd outgrow that, but I guess not."

Milo leaned in and folded his arms on the table like Finn, eyes sparkling more than polished silver. "Remember the time she begged Miss Willoughby to let us bury the dead frogs with dignity rather than dissect them? Or that time she turned you down at the square dance to dance with Peewee Hinkle despite that nasty cold he had? Claimed he was better looking than you even with that cherry nose and fever blister."

Laughter bubbled in Finn's throat, the memory of Liberty limping off the dance floor easing his lips into an all-out grin. "Yeah, she sure had blood in her eyes when I made fun of Hinkle that night." A chuckle slipped out. "Poor Peewee trailed her closer than a shadow after that, lovesick to the core."

"Yeah, poor slob …" Milo eyed him with a glint in his eye, the knowing look on his face blasting Finn's cheeks with an uncomfortable flash of fire.

Finn upended his coffee like it was 100-proof whiskey, gaze flicking across the room to where the ladies were just reentering through the back door. "The girls are back," he said, relief coursing as he mentally kicked himself for confiding in Parks in high school about his feelings for Liberty.

Jo Beth Templeton caught his eye from across the room, offering a coy smile and a wave as she and her best friend, Bettie Boswell—Milo's girl—made their way to the table.

Jo Beth was the girl Finn stepped out with the most—when he stepped out—which wasn't often, one of Milo's chief complaints. Pert near as pretty as Liberty, she was the only daughter of George Templeton, president of Virginia City's biggest bank, *and* the holder of Finn's note on his land.

Finn couldn't help but squirm a wee bit as he returned Jo Beth's smile with a stiff one of his own, wishing he didn't feel so darn guilty about squiring the banker's daughter. After all, he applied for and received the loan *long* before he'd begun seeing Jo Beth, but somehow Finn always sensed there were emotional strings attached. As if acquiring that loan committed him far more to Jo Beth than he ever wanted to be. Oh, he liked her well enough and certainly more than any of the other girls he stepped out with. But he made darn good and sure Jo Beth knew he wasn't beholden to any woman and that marriage was the *last* thing on his mind for a long time to come.

Say twenty, thirty years.

"I hired Liberty," Milo said, voice so low, Finn might have imagined it.

Finn blinked. *Make that the second last thing.*

Milo gave a slight shrug, his crooked smile bordering on an apology. "Just thought you should know, old buddy, since she'll be working three doors down from you day in and day out."

Eyes flicking to where Jo Beth and Bettie stopped to talk to a table of their friends, Finn bent in to hover low over his coffee cup, eyes as hard as the clamp of his jaw. "And just why in tarnation would you think I'd be interested in that, *old buddy?*"

Milo sighed and pushed his cup and saucer away, his smile veering toward dry. "Come on, Finn, you and I both know you've always had a thing for her, and I dare you to deny it."

It was a tossup over which was grinding more—Finn's

teeth or his stomach. "Yeah, I did, Parks, but that so-called 'thing' you allude to was a cold chill, my friend, nothing more."

"Or a warm one ..."

"Goodness me, sorry we took so long!" Jo Beth said with a little titter. She whooshed into the seat that Finn rose to pull out for her while Milo seated Bettie as well. Her blue eyes sparkled with mischief. "But Charlene had some juicy tidbits for us, didn't she, Bettie?"

Her best friend nodded, cheeks flushed with excitement as she leaned close, her voice lowering in volume. "Seems Charlene's mother saw Debbie Rhoades' beau in Carson City with another woman."

"And Doc Peters thinks Cheryl Herndon is going to have twins." Jo Beth giggled, offering Finn a shy smile.

"But the best news is ..." Bettie locked eyes with Jo Beth as the two of them shared a grin. "Liberty O'Shea is home from college, but not for long ..."

"What do you mean, 'not for long'?" Milo said, peering at Bettie through a squint while Finn chugged his water glass clear to the bottom. "I just hired her at the *Enterprise*, for pity's sake, so I doubt she's going anywhere soon."

"She is if her father has anything to say about it." Jo Beth wiggled her brows, raising her chin to eye the chalkboard menu on the wall. "She heard from Mary Lou Tanner, who heard from Kelly Reed Brown, who heard from a friend of Libby's cousin, that Libby and her father are butting heads again."

"Oh, now there's a headline for you," Finn muttered to Milo in a dry tone, Liberty's notorious rows with her father as common as dirt on Main Street.

Jo Beth paused to give Finn a teasing bat of her eyes. "My, but that peach pie with Flo's fresh-churned ice cream sounds awfully tempting, doesn't it, Finn?"

He laughed and shook his head, waving Flo over. "Not sure how you fit all that food in that tiny body, Miss Templeton, but it's a darn good thing your daddy gave me that loan."

"I know," she said with a flirty smile that drew his attention to her lush lips, one of the fringe benefits that had come along with the loan, unbeknownst to her father. She gave his arm a light squeeze. "But don't worry, Finn, there's plenty more where that came from …"

"Focus, Jo Beth," Milo said with a tight smile. "What are Libby and her father going 'round about now?"

Expelling a weary sigh that registered more than a bit of sarcasm towards her archrival, Jo Beth rolled her eyes. "Well, you know Liberty—more interested in a cause than a husband, so she flat out refused the proposal of a wealthy marital prospect in New York, handpicked by her daddy. A senator's son, no less, with aspirations to be a senator himself, and she turned him down flat." She wrinkled her nose. "Said she'd rather *be* a senator than marry one, if you can imagine that."

Somehow Finn could, and the thought coaxed a smile to his lips.

"Well, I can tell you right now that Liberty plans to stay because I just hired her at the paper after she begged for a chance to prove herself."

Jo Beth arched a brow. "Well, *that's* because her daddy cut off her allowance while she's home, according to Charlene," she said with a bit of a smirk, "a little leverage, if you will, but we all know how pig-headed Liberty can be."

Yes, we do … Finn flashed a smile when Flo moseyed over, ordering pie and more coffee for the table.

"Although I suspect in the end, her daddy will get his way," Jo Beth continued. "He usually does."

Finn frowned.

"Well, well," Jo Beth said softly, "speak of the devil."

Finn stopped breathing. A flash of heat jolted through his body at the sight of Liberty O'Shea in the doorway of Flo's Café with her best friends Kitty Jones and Martha Artyomenko. *The devil, indeed.* Complete with fiery hair and a pitchfork tongue. Not to mention the heat she evoked in his body every time he laid eyes on her. A smile rested on those luscious lips until her gaze lighted upon him, thinning her mouth considerably along with those green eyes the color of moss on a forest floor.

In a patch of poison ivy.

Flo approached them at the door, and Liberty's face eased into the sweet smile she awarded everyone but him. That is, until Flo began to lead them to the only empty table in the small café.

Right next to Finn's.

He couldn't help it—the blood siphoning from her usually rosy cheeks coaxed a grin to his lips, along with Flo's not-so-gentle tug of the little brat's arm when she reared back in a hard slant, feet fused to the floor like her shoes were made of glue. With Flo's firm grip and Kitty's gentle prod from behind, they succeeded in dragging her to the table, but not before Finn managed a roguish wink that helped replenish the blood in her face. "Why, hello there, Liberty Bell."

He casually slid an arm around Jo Beth's shoulders, knowing full well it would rile Liberty something fierce. She'd always accused him of being a lothario in school, and he took great pleasure in getting her goat. *Especially* after her father turned him down for a loan her senior year, accusing Finn of being a fortune hunter. Claimed his decision was based on the fact that "his Libby" didn't trust Finn, calling him "a skunk of a womanizer just like his father."

Finn had been so irate, he'd stood Libby up for the festival dance he'd finally gotten the nerve to ask her to, taking Jo Beth instead at the very last minute. His jaw hardened at the memory as he stared at the woman who had stabbed him straight through the heart. As sweet as you please during the time they spent together as festival volunteers, but then running back to Daddy to sully Finn's reputation. He released a silent sigh. He had to admit there were days he regretted the hurt he'd caused her that night, leaving her high and dry in front of the whole town.

But today sure wasn't one of them.

He casually fondled the lace on Jo Beth's scoop collar with blatant familiarity just to get on Libby's nerves. Delivering a lazy smile, he skimmed along Jo Beth's collarbone with the pad of his thumb. "Say, Miss Bell, you didn't happen to notice any starving babies or women outside, did you? 'Cause I sure would like to treat them to dinner ..."

Libby's eyes could have been jagged shards of emerald for all the daggers she was shooting his way. "I doubt Flo has nitroglycerin on the menu, Mr. McShane ..."

He grinned, adrenalin pumping through his veins at sparring with Liberty O'Shea once again. "Well, I don't know about that, Miss O'Shea, but Flo's chili pert near *'explodes'* on the tongue."

Her face flushed almost purple, and pleasure coursed through his bloodstream at being able to evoke some sort of emotion from this fire-haired beauty who haunted his dreams. As a God-fearing man, he knew he shouldn't take such joy in baiting one of God's own, but blue blazes, he never could help himself where Liberty O'Shea was concerned.

"You are pathetic, Mr. *McShame*, and I'm sure if you had a conscience, it would be as black as night." She turned away with a swoosh of that magnificent scarlet hair, and he grinned at Milo, who just shook his head, the smirk on his face stealing some of Finn's thunder.

"What was *that* all about?" Jo Beth said, never too happy when Finn paid attention to another woman, especially one she couldn't abide.

"Oh, just another one of Liberty's lost causes," he said loud enough for Liberty to hear. Heat crept up the back of his neck when the thought backfired with a painful cramp in his gut.

Just like me.

CHAPTER SIX

"YOU'RE ON TIME—I LIKE THAT, Miss O'Shea." Liberty's cheeks burned as she sent Milo Parks a polite smile, closing the door behind her before she calmly took a chair in front of his desk. Steers would fly before she'd let him know she'd been camped out at Flo's since sunup, drinking coffee nonstop while she peered at the glass door of the *Territorial Enterprise.* This job meant everything to her, and if she had to kiss Milo Parks' feet, she would, because she'd do anything to secure her future and that of the women of Nevada.

Finn McShane's cocky smile suddenly barged into her thoughts.

Well, almost anything.

"I believe in being on time, Mr. Parks," she said as demurely as she could, as if she were the employer and he merely the nauseous new employee whose knees felt like hog's-haw jelly.

"Good to hear. So, have you finished your editorial on the V&T Railroad?" Milo Parks appeared relaxed in his chair, the faintest of smiles hovering on his lips.

"Yes, sir, I have, and I hope it will meet with your approval." She removed her article from Papa's portfolio and handed it over, her unblinking gaze fused to his. For whatever reason, Milo Parks appeared to want to light a fire under his best friend, and Liberty was more than willing to comply.

Reaching to take the paper, he slanted back with a casual air.

Hands folded in her lap, she sat straight and tall on the edge of the chair, lungs deathly still while she watched his face. She had an itch on her nose, but refused to scratch it, determined to appear poised and confident despite the roiling in her gut. It wasn't until those full lips of his edged up in a genuine smile that she finally allowed herself to breathe, and when he laughed outright, her shoulders sank in relief. "You like it?"

He peered over the top of the paper and grinned. "I love it."

She chewed on the edge of her lip. "Do you think … it will stir things up? You know, as far as the plight of the Chinese?" she asked, desperate to expose the railroads for their despicable prejudice.

A deep laugh rumbled from his chest. "Oh, yeah, it'll stir things up all right." He tossed it back on his desk and chuckled. "And I have no idea about the Chinese."

"So I … have the job?" Voice tentative, she peered up from the edge of her seat, on tenterhooks that felt like a nest of Mama's knitting needles poking through a ball of yarn.

He studied her through pensive eyes despite the faint smile on his lips, elbows propped on the arms of his chair and hands folded. "Sure. Providing you're willing to start at the bottom."

If she scooted any closer to the edge, she'd be on the floor. "Oh, anything, Mr. Parks," she gushed with hands clasped to her mouth. "Absolutely anything and anytime—I am at your complete disposal."

"An apt choice of words, Miss O'Shea, because if you buck me on assignments I give, any 'disposal' will be yours—is that clear?"

"Oh, yes sir!" she breathed, hardly able to believe she had an honest-to-goodness job with an honest-to-goodness paycheck despite Papa's efforts to blackball her from employment in Virginia City. Never was she more grateful that the owner of the *Enterprise* was one of Papa's adversaries, untouchable by her father's money. She fought the rise of a smirk. *Let him put that in his pipe and puff it!*

"Good." Milo rifled through his side drawer for several seconds before producing an application, which he promptly slid across his desk. "Fill this out, give it to Viola at the front desk, and she'll cut you a paycheck every week. Hours are generally 7:00 to 5:00 unless you're on special assignment, then you stay till it gets done, understood?"

She nodded, quite sure she'd rather spend most of her time here than at Ponderosa Pines, where Papa bellowed nonstop over her "ungrateful suffragette ways." Her spirits dimmed a hair. Even if she did sorely miss Mama.

"You'll get paid 85 cents a day and 30 minutes for lunch."

The adrenaline coursing through her veins slowed to a crawl. "Eighty-five cents a day?"

He glanced up from a stack of notes he was rummaging through. "Is there a problem?"

"Uh …" Her chin rose. "Even the Chinese laborers on the horrific Central Pacific Railroad were paid a dollar a day, Mr. Parks."

His eyes narrowed despite the stiff smile on his face. "That's right, Miss O'Shea, and each and every one a man, so let's not get a bee in your bonnet."

Her mouth sagged open, wide enough for a whole hive of those blasted bees. "Excuse me, sir, but are you saying I'm to be paid less for the same work as a man just because I'm a woman?"

His eyes bore into hers like one of those confounded rotary drills they used to mine silver, but she didn't miss a twitch of a smile at the edge of his mouth. "*Now* you're getting the lay of the land, Miss O'Shea. So do you want the job or not?"

She slammed her mouth shut, teeth ground tight to keep

the piece of her mind from barreling out. Offering a curt nod, she jacked her chin even higher.

That infernal twitch of his smile bloomed like pigweed in a patch of petunias. "Good, then we have just one more business detail to cover." With a decidedly evil glint in his gaze that somehow brought to mind an outhouse and a skunk, Milo Parks shoved a paper and pen across his desk.

"What's this?" She slowly leaned in to study it, as if it were a scorpion about to strike. Her jaw dropped, near as wide as the mouth of the Comstock mine. As if starched by shock, her lashes rose in slow motion. "You want me to sign a contract?" she whispered, a tic fluttering in her temple, "to restrain my temper on the job?"

He nodded with a gleam of trouble in his eyes. "No matter the assignment, hour, or day. If you are on *Enterprise* business, you will keep that Irish temper under wraps or it and its owner will be out of a job, is that clear?"

Libby shot to her feet, her volume rising along with her. "This is blackmail! If I were a man, you would never do such a thing, Milo Parks." She stamped her kidskin boots. "This is bald-faced discrimination, and I will not stand for it!"

"Then *sit*," he said with a glare tempered by the ghost of a smile. "And it's not discrimination, Liberty, it's self-pres-ervation, and you darn well know it." He arched a brow when she stood there steaming. "I said *sit*. Or you can turn that mule-headed temper of yours around right now, Liberty O'Shea, and waltz out that door. Those are the terms—take 'em or leave 'em."

Hands knotted at her sides, she stood there glowering right back, body trembling with indignation along with the feathers on her hat. Jaw like rock, she slowly sucked in a calming breath. *All right, Liberty, just think of all the women you can help by holding your tongue ...* Huffing out her exas-peration, she plopped back in the chair, her anger cooling enough for regret to set in. "I ..." She swallowed the pride

clogging her throat. "I'm sorry," she rasped, gratified when
Milo gave her a sympathetic smile instead of pulling rank.
"I know you are, Liberty. Back in school, I've seen you
madder than a wet hornet with a headache when Finn and
I pulled some crazy stunt to drive *you* crazy, but in the end,
you always simmered down and did the right thing."

"Till the next time," she muttered, brows digging low.

Milo grinned. "Yeah, till the next time." His chest rose
and fell with a noisy sigh before he met her gaze with a
truce of a smile that put her at ease. "The truth is, Liberty,
I like you—always have—and Finn likes you too."

An unladylike grunt parted from her lips. "Sure, Finn
likes me all right—as long as I'm in another state."

He grinned while he scratched the back of his head.
"No, he does, really, it's just that …"

Her eyelids narrowed. "It's just what?"

"It's just that he's my best friend and more of a brother,
you know? And with the V&T office just three doors
away …"

"You want us to avoid killing each other," she said, finishing his thought.

A boyish smile slid across his face. "Something like that."

Her ruffled bodice expanded with air, and she expelled
it again in one, arduous exhale. "All right, Mr. Parks, you
have my word I will do everything in my power to get
along with Mr. *McVain*." Smile flat, she studied the contract
in its entirety before scrawling her name across the bottom
line. Laying the pen aside, she pushed the paper forward,
lips in a twist. "After all, shouldn't be too hard if I stay as
far away from him as humanly possible, right?"

"Yeah, well, about that …" Milo cocked his head, brows
dipped as he drew air through clenched teeth.

The smile froze on her face.

"The *Enterprise* is one of the biggest sponsors for the
annual Fourth of July Festival as you know …"

"Yesssss …" she said slowly, her vision thinning significantly.

"Well, I'm the co-chairman of the planning committee, so we're going to need your help. Figured I'd have you co-chair with me as your first assignment."

"Okay …" The breath she'd been holding slowly seeped out. "That doesn't sound too bad so far, if writing's still involved."

"Oh, absolutely," Milo assured her with a forceful nod of his head. "Anything you care to contribute that factors into the patriotic theme of our fair city or state—features, editorials, newsy updates, whatever. As long as the festival planning doesn't suffer, the sky's the limit."

A grin pulled at her lips. "You know, this could actually be fun—getting paid to chair the festival. I mean, I've always loved it—the booths, the baking contest, the dance, the parade."

"And don't forget the fireworks," Milo said with a smile, folding her signed contract and tucking it in his pocket.

Liberty clasped her hands together, suddenly as giddy as a toddler staring at spider flashes of fire in a dark and smoky sky. "Oh, yes, the fireworks," she breathed, heart near bursting like the gunpowder rockets that would spiral to the stars. "There are few things I love more than fireworks."

A lazy grin tipped Milo's mouth as he handed her several more sheets. "That's good. Here's the lead on a story I'd like you to tackle, along with the festival notes Viola typed up for this year and last. You know, just to give you ideas before the meeting at City Hall tonight at seven."

Liberty jumped to her feet and took the sheets before extending her hand across the desk. "Thank you so much, Mr. Parks, for entrusting me with such an exciting project."

Milo pumped her hand with gusto, the glimmer in his eye no doubt matching the sparkle in her own. "My pleasure, Liberty—I think you're the perfect person for the job, especially given your love of fireworks."

"Oh, yes, sir," she agreed with matched enthusiasm, "fireworks are one of my most favorite things in the whole, wide world."

"That's real good to hear," he said with a broad grin that was instantly followed by a wink. "'Cause I guarantee you, Miss O'Shea—you're going to see plenty."

CHAPTER SEVEN

"WHOA, BOY." FINN SLOWED HIS horse's brisk gait as they neared City Hall, his painted palomino obviously intent on barreling through town to Finn's acreage instead. Couldn't blame him, though—Finn spent every free moment working on his land, clearing trees or building his cabin. Reining Lightning in, he slid off the saddle and tied him to the post outside of City Hall, a small but impressive brick building at the edge of town where all city business was conducted. Lightning nickered as light peeked out of a bank of windows on either side, illuminating scrubby-looking bushes and a wagon wheel crawling with trumpet vine.

With a click of his tongue, Finn fished two apple cores from his pocket and fed it to his best buddy, the remains of a rushed dinner after working his land for several hours. Returning home at dusk, he'd barely had time for a quick washup and shave before bolting out again, stomach rumbling over the smell of pot roast his mother had made. "Save me a plate," he'd said on his way out the door, bussing his mother's cheek along with his sister's. Following a quick tousle of both his little brothers' shaggy hair, he'd grabbed two apples on the way. "And don't wait up—Milo and I have a lot of planning to do after the meeting."

Looking for more handouts, Lightning nudged Finn's chambray shirt, which was thankfully free of the awful tie he was forced to wear during the day as a representative of theV&T. He was a simple man with simple tastes, one who preferred faded denim and dusty cowhide boots to fancy suits and spit-polished shoes. But he'd learned to bite the bullet and dress the part of a dandy if he wanted to own his land free and clear sooner rather than later. *During the day, that is.* The nights were all his to dress and live as he liked, chipping away at all that stood in the path of his dream to own the largest cattle spread in Nevada.

"Don't worry, little buddy," he said softly, as much to himself as the fawn-and-white-colored animal he'd trained from a colt, "patience is a silver mine all its own, so there's more treats ahead." With one final scratch behind Lightning's ear, Finn slowly mounted the wooden steps to the fancy double doors the mayor's wife just *had* to have. Passing a hand through his damp hair, he reached for the brass knob, lips tipping in a smile at the sound of Miss Willoughby's good-natured bickering with Deputy Poke.

The squabbling filtered down a narrow hall from the back of the building, their long-standing feud always reminding him of a married couple. He grinned and shook his head as he made his way to the public meeting room. Leroy Poke needed to wake up and court the schoolteacher good and proper, even if it meant the end of her teaching career.

"Well, it's about bloomin' time one of the co-chairs showed up," Harvey Sullivan groused, the barrel-chested sawmill owner who was always thirty minutes early everywhere he went. "Thought I had the wrong blasted night."

"Oh, frog spit, Harvey Sullivan," Mrs. Poppy said with a heft of a chubby chin, silver and snow-white hair piled high in a donut bun as lopsided as her sweet smile. Married to Pastor Horace Poppy for over fifty years, Clara Poppy was as eccentric—and outspoken—as they came, but a mainstay in Virginia City. *And* one of the few who could put "Sully" in his place. Her knitting needles were flying, clacking right along with Harvey's ill-fitting dentures, a clicking habit old Harv had whenever he was impatient.

Which was pretty much all of the time.

"Meetings start at eight," she said, "and Griffin is ten minutes early, so just button up, young man." Her blue eyes sparkled as she flashed a bright smile at Finn, her moon face so full, there was nary a wrinkle despite her seventy-five years. "Evenin' Griffin. You got that land cleared yet?" she said with a sassy wink. "Kinda hankerin' for a wedding, young man, so it may as well be you." A twinkle lit her rheumy blue eyes as she peeked up from her knitting. "Been praying real hard one of you young bucks would get a move on and settle down."

Finn laughed, the sound bouncing off the plastered walls along with several male chuckles, including Pastor Poppy's, who patted his wife's arm. "Better run for your life, son. When Mrs. Poppy puts her mind to prayer, there's no stopping her *or* the Almighty."

Tossing his Stetson on the empty seat beside him, Finn shifted one of the chairs in the first row and straddled it, grinning ear to ear. "That's okay, Pastor. Gotta feeling those prayers are gonna be answered by old Milo soon enough."

"Well, pop another pearl onto St. Peter's Gate," Mrs. Poppy said with a girlish giggle, "he did seem to be awfully cozy with Bettie Boswell at the ice cream social, as I recall."

"Yes, ma'am," Finn said with a devious smile, figuring his best friend deserved a little payback after siccing Liberty O'Shea on him last week. He measured a thin strip of air with forefinger and thumb. "The boy's this close to popping the question, so you best focus all those prayers on him."

Emitting a tiny squeal, Miss Willoughby palmed her hands in prayer mode, brown eyes dancing as much as Mrs. Poppy's. "Oh, that's *so* exciting," she said with a dreamy look. "Nothing makes me happier than a wedding!"

"Mmm … hear that, Deputy Poke?" Mrs. Poppy turned her sights on the poor deputy, whose freckled face turned redder than the field of poppies in the old woman's back-

yard. She jiggled silver brows. "Wilhelmina *loves* wed
-dings ..."

The slam of the front door saved poor Miss Willoughby,
whose deep blush bypassed Deputy Poke's by several
shades, the timely arrival of more meeting attendees a welcome diversion. Virginia City's mayor burst into the room
with all the force of a 12-pound Howitzer. His deep voice
boomed as puffs of smoke billowed from a Cuban cigar
while his secretary and an entourage of others followed
close behind. Although short in stature, Mayor Charlie Tuttle cut a fine, if somewhat bulky, figure in a single-breasted
frock coat and silk vest.

Marching right up to a table with a makeshift podium
and two chairs at the front of the room, he glanced at
his pocket watch before pounding his gavel. "Let's start
this meeting, shall we?" He peered at the group of people
occupying the first two rows, eyes in a squint. "Where's
your co-chair, Finn?"

Finn righted his chair to face the front with the others
and sat, leg cocked on his knee and hands latched behind
his neck. "Said he might be detained a few minutes, Mayor.
Something about a proposal he was putting together for
J.T., or some such nonsense."

Mrs. Poppy's chuckle was rich and low. "You sure it
wasn't for Miss Boswell?"

Finn gave her a wink. "Could be."

Slam! Several pair of footsteps clattered down the hallway before Milo rushed in with a satchel over his shoulder
and a briefcase in his hand. "My apologies, Mayor, but J.T.
was on one of his jaw benders, which is why both of us
are late."

Both of us? Finn's eyes narrowed at the swish and peek of
a skirt behind Milo's broad frame, and his blood instantly
ran cold. *Oh, no, he wouldn't ...*

"Why, good evening, Liberty," Mrs. Poppy said with a
pleased lift of brows. Her knitting needles paused for the

very first time as she glowed at Liberty O'Shea with a smile brighter than the blasted candles in the chandelier overhead. "I didn't know you were on the planning committee."

Liberty nodded her hellos to everyone while Finn forced himself to breathe. She awarded Mrs. Poppy with a hug and her most affectionate smile. "Mrs. Poppy! So good to see you again, and yes, Mr. Parks hired me at the *Enterprise*, so he's solicited my help for the festival."

While Liberty chattered on with Mrs. Poppy and Miss Willoughby, Finn shot Milo a look that should have singed his friend's ears, but Milo only grinned and plopped down in the seat beside him. "Evenin', Finn."

"Don't evenin' me, Parks. What the devil is she doing here?" he hissed under his breath.

"She's assisting me, old buddy, *and* you."

Finn stifled a grunt. "I don't want her anywhere near me, much less assisting me, you clown, and you know that." He fought off a shiver, as much from her proximity as the notion of dealing with the woman's prickly nature.

Bam! Bam! Bam! "Looks like everyone's here," the mayor said with a noisy bang of his gavel, "so let's get this train on the tracks and chugging full speed ahead, eh, Finn?" He chuckled, obviously amused by his attempt at humor, which Finn didn't share in the least. "But before I introduce our co-chairs, let me say that as the richest city in America, we have an obligation to put on a Fourth of July celebration that will blow the socks off everyone in town." He gave the audience a wink. "Not to mention the government dignitaries who will be in attendance and the city's esteemed investors from our sister city, San Francisco. That said, this year I'm looking for bigger and better to celebrate the kickoff into Virginia City's tenth year as a city. I want this year's charity fundraiser to beat all those we've had in the past, so let's not be shy with suggestions, all right?" He homed in on Milo. "I trust you have last year's notes and records of expenses and profits?"

Milo hefted the saddlebag in the air. "Yes, sir, right here. Also, my assistant, Liberty O'Shea, was kind enough to put together a preliminary schedule of events, just as a starting point, of course, with copies for everyone."

"Excellent, Milo, and a nod of appreciation to Liberty for pitching in."

A pretty blush dusted Liberty's cheeks as she offered a nervous smile, rising to hand out a typed schedule to each person in the room. She ended with Finn, whose paper somehow slipped from her hand to land on the floor. "Whoops … sorry, Mr. McShane," she said in an innocent tone that he seriously doubted.

I'll just bet you are. Finn managed a stiff smile as he retrieved his copy.

"I'd like to thank our two co-chairs Milo Parks and Finn McShane for volunteering so much of their time to this worthy effort. *And* to Pastor and Mrs. Poppy for allowing us to use their farm as our venue. Then, of course, to Harvey Sullivan for providing all the lumber needed for booth and float construction, and to my own secretary, Miss Mimi Baker, for recording the minutes of tonight's meeting. And finally, I applaud each of you fine citizens for becoming involved in what I hope will be the highlight of our year. Without further ado, I turn the floor over to our co-chairs to get the ball rolling." The mayor moved to tap the back of both Finn's and Milo's chairs. "Gentlemen, if you'll take over center stage, Mr. Parks can start us off."

As the numbers man, Milo wasted no time reviewing the details of last year's festival, the pros, the cons, the expenses, the profits, and how those profits were spent. From there, Finn took over, systematically discussing each item on a detailed meeting list he'd put together earlier in the week. Following a vote on whether to retain, delete, or add to prior activities, he then offered creative suggestions for new fundraisers, sparking a lively debate. Within an hour and a half, budgets were set and committee chairs established, along with a jam-packed July third and fourth two-day agenda. From a talent show, picnic auction, hayride, and baking contest, to a bake sale, horse race, potluck dinner, barn dance, and fireworks, the stage was set for a Fourth of July festival second to none.

With a quick glance at his checklist to make sure he'd covered every detail, Finn finally tucked it back in his pocket with a satisfied smile. "Well that about covers everything on my list, so anybody have anything to add before we wrap up for the night?"

"Ahem." Milo rose with a gruff clear of his throat, avoiding eye contact with Finn. "Actually, the newest member of the *Territorial Enterprise*, Miss Liberty O'Shea, has some new and pretty exciting ideas she'd like to share, so I'm going to turn my chair over to her."

Finn's body went to ice as Liberty rose with a stack of papers clutched to her chest, her presence at the podium freezing the smile on his face as stiff as sagebrush in a Nevada blizzard.

"Thank you, everyone, for your time because I know we're all anxious to go home, but I promise I'll make it brief."

Brief. Smile about to crack, Finn scorched Milo with a mental threat. *Like Parks' life is about to be ...*

"I applaud Mr. McShane for some excellent ideas that I think will provide a very decent start to our fundraising efforts."

Decent start? Finn's gaze swung from lacerating Milo to gaping at the petite woman beside him, who stood with shoulders square and head high like it was one of those blasted spelling bees in which they'd always butted heads.

"I cannot express just how proud I am of our great city and how honored I am to be on this committee. Not only is Virginia City one of the largest cities in the West, but she is also one of the most important, a beacon of civic leadership and a true trailblazer. I believe a city with that level of power and prominence should have a fundraiser to match, don't you? With that in mind, I've taken the liberty"—she paused to render a shy smile to an audience who seemed rapt with attention—"no pun intended—to put together a proposal that will garner community support well beyond picnic auctions and bake sales, as wonderful as those activities may be."

She offered Finn a token nod before she handed out her flyers, returning to the podium to elaborate on each point with the same poise and efficiency she'd always demonstrated in school. Her excitement appeared contagious given the sparkles of interest in everyone's eyes.

It was everything Finn could do to keep his jaw from dangling, the litany of truly remarkable ideas bruising his cheeks with a heat that torched both his temper and his pride. From the creation of a festival memorial catalog with ads placed by local merchants, to a "Merchant of the Year" award based on highest donation, the little brat made his own efforts look like child's play. Her idea of a themed booth contest was sheer genius, where both the public and businesses could promote a cause or product to the residents of Virginia City, visiting dignitaries, and hundreds of visitors from all over the state.

From distributing flyers to stores all over Nevada, to posting ads in various newspapers across the state and those nearby, she'd covered promotion of the event as well, every jot and tittle with her usual annoying precision. Even Finn had to admit the ideas were nothing short of brilliant. Especially the award for the winning booth, where the winner not only received a cash prize, but won the title of king or queen of the festival as well, with their own float in the parade.

Oh, and a front-page feature article in the *Enterprise* to further promote the winner's own business or cause.

Finn's teeth ground tight. And he had *no* doubt whatsoever if Liberty came in first, the V&T would come in last, because she'd surely stir up more grief for both the railroad *and* for him.

IF she won …

Which meant he and the V&T had to make darn sure she didn't …

"And finally, I hope I've saved the best for last …" She reached into her portfolio for a scroll of paper.

Finn blinked. *Blue blazes, there's MORE???*

Pausing to inhale deeply, Liberty cast a tentative look around the room, her manner nervous as she clutched the scroll to her chest, teeth tugging at that lush lower lip. "I have no doubt that when this Fourth of July festival fundraiser is over, the memories will live on forever for each and every one of us." She lifted a hand to touch a finger to her temple with a shy smile. "Up here. But wouldn't it be wonderful if something more tangible would live on as well? Something we could see with our eyes and cherish with our hearts?"

Bodice expanding with another intake of air, she slowly unrolled the scroll. Several gasps parted from the ladies' lips as Liberty held up an exquisite watercolor painting of a modest town square. Comprised of a desert rock and paver courtyard smack dab in front of City Hall, it was simple but impressive. A stately pine tree graced the far center while two smaller Nevada flowering bushes in terra cotta planters flanked a park bench on each side of the square. In the midst of it all a flagpole stood proudly with an American flag furling in the breeze, and Finn's throat immediately swelled with pride.

"As you can see from the painting, I propose a modest beginning for a town square to which we can add every year with flowers or trees or even a grandstand for future city functions. With our desert wealth of flagstone rocks and bushes, the cost would be minimal, but the pride and beauty it could bring"—she paused for effect, her voice almost pulsing with excitement—"would be monumental. This year we could shoot our festival fireworks off in the hill beyond, providing an excellent vantage point from which to watch, and we can even decorate the pine at Christmas. This is only my humble suggestion of what the square could include, of course, subject to committee input. But I've already spoken to Zeb Miller and his sons, and they've offered to build the square at cost beginning immediately if the board approves a plan," she finished with a hopeful gleam in her eyes.

Stunned silence reined for several seconds until Mayor Tuttle shot to his feet with a tremendous ovation echoed by everyone in the room. "Well, now, that's one dandy of a presentation, young lady, if I say so myself. Finn, let's take the vote and get this buggy rolling."

Finn lumbered to his feet like an old man, his smile as tight as his gut. "Well now, I'd like to talk this through one moment, Mayor, before we go and bite off more than we can chew. While I agree that was one fine presentation by Miss O'Shea"—he managed a wooden nod at Liberty, whose patient air galled him all the more—"grand ideas like this require grand planning and way more man hours than we can afford with a sparse number of volunteers and a mere two co-chairs—"

"Uh … three co-chairs," Milo said carefully, avoiding Finn's eyes as he rose to his feet. He scratched the back of his neck with a sheepish smile. "Truth is, J.T.'s a little worried about me spending so much time away from the paper, so Liberty agreed to lend us a hand."

A hand. Finn blinked when a memory flashed of that same "hand" pinching and pummeling his back while she kicked and thrashed over his shoulder.

"But …" Milo said with a quick raise of his palm, as if to quell Finn's mood, "rest assured Liberty already has a detailed plan in place for each of the points in her presentation, so you can breathe easy, Finn."

Breathe easy? Blue blistering blazes, he couldn't breathe at all …

"Excellent plan, Co-chairman Parks," the mayor said with a hearty shake of Milo's hand, sealing Finn's fate with a quick vote that confirmed both Liberty's appointment as co-chair and her docket of ideas. The mayor then pumped her hand in a downright nauseating show of approval while everyone else in the room rushed to congratulate her like she was the bloomin' Well's Fargo wagon.

When the crowd finally thinned, Finn had no choice but to step up and take his medicine like a man. Searing Milo with a thin-lipped glare, he offered Liberty a shake of his hand. "Congratulations, Miss O'Shea, for stealing the show tonight. Should be interesting putting our heads together once again."

The press of those perfectly pink lips assured him she was just as reluctant as he, her tone and smile as cool as his own. "I don't believe we ever 'put our heads together' before, Mr. McShane—butt them together, yes—but little else. However, if they can drill through a mountain to mine silver, you and I can certainly drill through our prior differences to glean gold for our fair city." A russet brow angled in warning. "As long as we limit all sparks to the fireworks, we should be just fine."

"Fine?" Milo slapped Finn on the back, apparently secure in the assumption that Finn wouldn't rip his tonsils out in front of the mayor and Liberty. "Nope, better than fine—you two will make a formidable team, eh, Mayor?"

"No question 'bout that," Mayor Tuttle said with a broad smile, snatching his bowler from a chair while giving Finn a knowing wink. "Yesiree, young man, gotta feeling this little filly here is gonna keep you on your toes."

"Yeah, that's what I'm afraid of," Finn mumbled as he snatched his own hat from the table, uttering a silent prayer for patience.

And on my knees.

CHAPTER EIGHT

"**B**ISCUIT, DEAR?" LIBERTY'S MOTHER PASSED the basket to Liberty's best friend Kitty, her smile as warm as their cook Gertie's buttermilk biscuits, hot out of the oven. At forty-five years of age, Maeve O'Shea was an older version of Liberty with auburn curls threaded with silver and restrained in a proper coif at the back of her head. She reached to squeeze Kitty's hand. "It's so nice having you over for dinner again, Kitty, although I wish Martha could have joined us too. It's been a bit dull here since Liberty's been away at school."

"Likewise, I assure you, Mrs. O'Shea." Kitty shot a broad smile at Liberty. "Especially the 'dull' part now that Libby's back home." She wiggled her brows. "Nobody stirs the pot like our Libby."

"Humpf." Her father chomped on a roll. "The only pots stirring in this house will be in the kitchen, as it should be."

A gentle sigh drifted from Libby's lips as her mother reached to give her hand a reassuring squeeze, letting her daughter know she was not alone in her dreams of liberty for all. As much as Libby loved New York, coming home to her mother was a salve to her soul, even *if* she and her father didn't see eye-to-eye on the direction of her life. At least her mother understood her need for independence, the burning desire to make a difference.

Before her mother had married her father, Maeve Monroe had been a strong-willed New York socialite on the ground floor of the suffragette movement. At least until Grandpa Monroe had forced her to marry Aiden O'Shea in a business alliance between two of New York's wealthiest banking families. Although Mama had reluctantly acquiesced to both her father and her new husband, that hadn't stopped her from raising her one and only daughter to be an independent thinker.

Much to Papa's dismay.

Kitty shot a polite smile in Aiden's direction, her dark curls gathered back in a chignon that made her look so much older than Libby remembered. "Well, all stirring aside, Mr. O'Shea, it's certainly good to have my best friend home again."

"So, Kitty," Liberty's father said, voice gruff in his typical no-nonsense manner. His dark moustache twitched in annoyance as he reached for his coffee. "I presume you'll be volunteering for the festival committee as well?" Bushy brows beetled low as his gaze flicked from Kitty to Libby and back while he peered over the rim of his cup. "If so, I certainly hope it's on the quilting or baking committee instead of trying to run the show like my girl here."

"Liberty is a co-chair, Aiden," her mother emphasized with the barest lift of her chin, sidestepping her husband's question to Kitty altogether. Her tone was taut despite the smile on her face, revealing a hint of the one sore spot in an otherwise healthy marriage. "Which means she shares responsibilities with two others, darling, both males."

"I prefer the term 'mules,'" Liberty muttered for Kitty's ears alone, fighting a smile when a giggle slipped from her best friend's lips.

Papa grunted. "Poppycock! Women belong in the home, Maeve, tending to their husbands and children, not trying to elbow their way into a man's world." His mouth skewed to the right in a dry smile that reflected the delicate balance her parents had forged between affection and opinion. "But apparently you raised a daughter as stubborn as the bride I married over thirty years ago, with a backbone of steel to match and a passel of pig-headed pride."

"Yes, darling, I did," Mama said with a glint in her eye that sparkled with both humor and grit. "And one of these days, Aiden O'Shea, I will get you to admit that I have saved you from a life of utter boredom with that very backbone of steel and pigheaded pride. Which, by the way, my love"—the glint shone to a gleam—"pales next to my husband's."

"I'll vouch for that." Libby winked at her father.

Her tease earned a rare chuckle as he relented with a shake of his head. "Pure self preservation, my dear, granted by the Almighty, no doubt, in lieu of a son." His smile tipped as he buttered another roll. "And don't think I won't be having words with Him in the hereafter, as to the wisdom of surrounding me with stubborn females."

"*If* you go to the right hereafter, darling," her mother said with a squirm of a smile.

"I'll second that." Their beloved cook and housekeeper, Gertie, barreled into the elegant dining room with a tray of her famous lemon meringue pie, her look as sour as the dessert. She clunked plates down in front of everyone at the table, a tossup as to which slid more lopsided—the meringue on the pie or the silver bun atop her head. The new French maid uniform Papa insisted she wear seemed out of place on her tall lanky frame, especially given the insult of cowboy boots she wore just to get Papa's goat. "Specially after the sin of forcing me to wear this high-fa-lutin' Frenchie getup." Gertie sloshed coffee in Papa's cup with her usual crabby air, her trademark since Mama had begged Papa to hire her as their housekeeper years ago, insisting that being a chuck-wagon cook for uncouth cowboys was no place for a lady.

A point on which both Mama and Papa strongly disagreed.

Ignoring Gertie's mood, her father refocused on Kitty,

lifting a cup that dripped coffee from the pool of liquid in his saucer, compliments of his disgruntled cook. "Please tell me, Kitty, that you've volunteered for something more feminine than trying to push your way into a man's world like my suffragette daughter."

"Unfortunately for me, Papa," Liberty said with a resigned sigh, "Kitty's father feels the way you do about females in leadership roles, so all he'll allow Kitty to do is help me with my booth."

"Humpf." Papa unbuttoned his pinstriped vest to make room for Gertie's pie. "At least *somebody* has control of his daughter." He glanced up as Gertie headed to the kitchen. "Gertie, I'll have a touch of whiskey in my—" The swinging door whooshed closed, deflating his gruff manner in a weary expulsion of air. "And hopefully control of their maid."

"What booth?" Mama wanted to know, quickly sidetracking Papa's request for alcohol, something she had secretly instructed Gertie to ignore.

Liberty proceeded to expound on the ideas she'd suggested to the festival committee, their enthusiastic response, and her vision for a booth of her own.

"Why, darling, that sounds wonderful!" The flush of pride in Mama's face was evident in the glow of her green eyes and the eager press of her palms, dessert all but forgotten. "And I'm so grateful Mr. Parks is allowing time on your new job to work on the festival, because you certainly have a lot to do."

"No business working a job in the first place," Papa grumbled, gouging his pie.

"So, Libby, hear tell Finn McShane is one of your co-chairs." Kitty spooned a bite of dessert in her mouth with a secret smile. "That alone should be good for a fair share of the fireworks, don't you think?"

"What?" Papa's spoon froze mid-air, jaw distended. "You mean to tell me you'll be working with that McShane hoodlum?" He slammed his fork to his plate, cheeks ruddy above lips now compressed to near white.

"Now, Aiden—" Mama's tone reverted to soothing mode.

"Don't 'now, Aiden' me, Maeve—I don't want that scalawag around my daughter. The boy's not from good stock, I tell you. His father was nothing but a drunk with a powder-keg temper who took it out on his family, then picked a fight with pert near every man in this town." He jabbed a fork into his pie, his scowl deepening considerably. "Blasted Irish Protestant. Nothing but a low-life lush, I tell you, who up and ran away with a saloon girl, leaving his family to wallow like pigs in poverty."

"All the more reason to respect the boy, Aiden," Mama said softly, "because he's made something of himself despite his tragic upbringing. And Protestant or Catholic, darling—the good Lord loves us all."

Papa slammed a palm on the table. "He's nothing but a womanizer and fortune hunter, I tell you. Selling his soul to George Templeton, no doubt sealing the deal by courting his daughter. Just like he tried to do with Liberty, but I was too smart for him."

"He's courting Jo Beth?" Libby blinked several times, unpleasantly surprised at the sudden cramp in her chest. She'd seen them together at Flo's, of course, but she hadn't realized they were an actual couple. Her mood suddenly turned as acidic as Gertie's lemon meringue pie.

"Not according to Finn," Kitty said, gulping down more dessert, "and he makes no bones about it. But I will say he steps out with Jo Beth more than any other girl in town, so I guarantee both Jo Beth and her father have high expectations. *Especially* since Mr. Templeton loaned Finn the money for his land."

"They're all in cahoots," Papa said with a growl, pushing his empty plate away to level a finger at Libby. "First that no-good scoundrel gives the V&T's business to Templeton, then he ups and buys Lester Calloway's prime land across the river, which everyone knows I've had my eye on forever."

Mama took a sip of her coffee. "Really, Aiden, it's common knowledge the V&T loan decision was based on George's connections with V&T brass, so I don't know how you can blame poor Finn—"

"*Poor* Finn?" Papa's eyes bulged in shock. "For the love of decency, woman, he's courting the daughter of the man who gave him that blasted loan."

Mama's smile hardened a hair, a sure sign Papa was beginning to ruffle her ire. "As Kitty reminded us and as *everyone* in town knows, Finn is *not* courting Jo Beth. And might I remind you that Finn came to *you* for that loan first? A loan on which *you* turned him down, if you recall, Aiden O'Shea, so that boy had no choice but to go to George Templeton's bank."

Her chin notched up as she stirred more cream in her coffee. "And as far as that prime land 'everyone' knows you've had your eye on, everyone also knows you lost that land through your own bullheaded pride, always trying to bully poor Lester into a sale for *less* than the land was worth. So don't be pinning that on Finn McShane either. Besides," she said with a tight smile, a subtle indication she was reaching her limit with Papa's vendetta against Finn McShane. "I always liked the boy when he visited Marge's son Milo during our quilting bees. So personable and polite to everyone, although I know he did pick on Libby a time or two."

"A time or two?" Libby gaped at her mother, hardly able to believe she was siding with Finn *McPain*. "Papa's right—he's a hooligan who made my life miserable in school, and you're defending him?"

"So, Liberty darling," Mama said with a pleasant smile, apparently anxious to steer the conversation as far away from Finn McShane as possible. "Have you come up with a theme for your booth?"

Expelling a noisy sigh, Libby was grateful for the change of subject. In no time, her excitement bubbled back up as she shared her plans for an "education" booth that she hoped would educate Virginia City on women's rights as well as other subjects of interest. "And Miss Willoughby is helping us with the booth," Libby finished with a contented sigh, "by lending her portable chalkboard, books, and bookcases, so we can decorate it like a real school."

"And don't forget about the apple-bobbing game," Kitty said with a proud lift of her chin, "since every booth is required to have a game to draw parents and children alike."

Mama clapped her hands, Libby's and Kitty's enthusiasm obviously catching. "Girls, that sounds wonderful! If Papa or I can help in any way, just let us know." She allowed a conciliatory smile in Papa's direction. "Before Papa made his fortune in banking, you know, he was fairly handy with tools, so I'm sure he'll be happy to oblige if you need him to hammer anything."

"Especially if it's Finn McShane," Papa muttered, earning a stiff arch of Mama's brow.

"Speaking of which …" Kitty leaned in, arms crossed on the table as she eyed Libby with a glint of trouble. "I'm guessing Finn's theme will be "transportation," which certainly fits given his job with the V&T. Heaven knows he's been able to railroad anybody and anything with that smile since he was knee-high to a toadstool." Mischief curled on her lips. "Especially Jo Beth."

Papa rose and tossed his napkin on his plate, his scowl a mirror image of Libby's.

"Mmm …" Tempering her smile, Mama patted the napkin to her mouth, the barest hint of tease in her tone as she pushed back her chair. "Looks like you'll be butting heads with that boy one last time, Liberty darling, so hopefully when it comes to the education booth, some of the tutelage will be his."

Kitty's throaty chuckle echoed as she shoveled in the last of her dessert, licking the spoon with a definite twinkle in her eye. "If he doesn't 'railroad' her first."

CHAPTER NINE

PARKS, YOU ARE IN A heap of horse biscuits! Finn ripped his copy of the *Territorial Enterprise* in two and then again, crumpling the pieces into a wad big enough to choke his best friend. He issued a grunt. Not to mention his brand-new "assistant," who'd just tarred and feathered him on the editorial page of Virginia City's most prestigious newspaper. Jaw grinding, he hurled the paper ball across the meeting room in City Hall, missing the wastebasket in the corner by a mile.

And I'm supposed to co-chair a committee with these people?

His stomach growled as he glanced at the clock on the wall, wishing he'd had time to go home for dinner first or grab a quick meal at Flo's before the weekly festival meeting. But the bigwigs from V&T had been in today, so there'd been no time to eat anything but an apple and peruse the paper while he waited for his co-chairs.

No … make that co-enemies.

Slander and starvation. Not a good combination for a guy whose almost nonexistent temper had been doused with kerosene by a traitorous best friend and a sassy suffragist. Determined to remain calm, he stood and retrieved the crumpled paper, absently lobbing it back and forth while he sauntered to his seat, derailing his frustration by thinking of his land instead. He was almost done clearing the section for the house and could start building a small cabin soon before plotting out the split-rail fence he planned to build in the west pasture.

The front door of City Hall opened and closed.

"Finally," Finn muttered, tossing the paper ball onto the table before pulling his notes and a pad of paper from his satchel. The hard click of heels echoed down the hallway, and he glanced up to see Liberty march into the room like she owned it. The full skirt of her green silk dress swished with authority and pert near more ribbons, bows, and fringe than the ladies' department of Mort's Mercantile.

Mouth suddenly dry, Finn's renegade gaze betrayed him with a slow body scan of the girl who wreaked havoc with his pulse. From the rich auburn curls piled at the back of her head to the creamy complexion that reminded him of his mama's buttermilk roses, she was a true beauty. His eyes skimmed down the shapely bodice that narrowed into a tiny waist, only to swell again into generous hips a mite fuller than the scrawny girl he used to taunt.

Heat singed the back of his neck when he realized he was staring, and deeply ingrained manners launched him to his feet, forcing him to rise, along with his hackles. Blue thunder, he hadn't even known he had hackles until that woman sailed into town. "Where's Parks?" he said in a gruff tone far too short. At six-foot-three, he'd always been long on height, patience, and personality, but since Liberty O'Shea's return to Virginia City, he'd been whittled down to size.

"Good evening to you, too, Mr. McShane," she said with a professional air that got on his last nerve.

"That's debatable. Where's Parks?"

"He's running late and asked that we get started." She systematically placed her hat, reticule, and portfolio on the table and pulled out a chair, sliding in with the same grace and ease he remembered from school. The gentle scent of lilacs drifted in the air, a taunt that reminded him of the day he'd carried her to Parks' office. Immediately his blood heated at the memory of her body against his, feather light and womanly soft. His lips went flat. *Except for those blasted steel toes and iron knees.*

Removing her notepad from what looked to be a brand-new leather portfolio, she positioned it just so in front of her before shimmying to the edge of her chair. She folded her hands on top. "Mr. McShane ..." Her eyes actually softened, the color of trees awakening in the spring, a watercolor wash of the purest, lightest green he'd ever seen. "Finn," she said quietly, her voice just above a whisper as her head dipped the slightest bit, allowing those deadly eyes to peek up beneath a fringe of dark lashes. "Since we're going to be working together so closely for the next few months, I would very much like to be friends."

"Friends." His terse response bore the weight of his skepticism.

Her chin elevated the barest amount, tempered by the faintest of smiles. "Yes, friends, a totally foreign concept to you when it comes to women, I realize, Mr. McShane. But who knows—you might find you like the benefits of intelligent conversation and total honesty."

"I doubt that," he muttered, still riled over the scathing article she'd written about him and the V&T. Scrubbing his face with his palms, he huffed out a heavy sigh and finally extended his hand. "All right, why not?" he said with a smile as flat as his mood. "Maybe it'll earn me better press in the *Enterprise*."

She had the grace to blush as she rose to slowly reach for his proffered hand, hesitating inches away as if it were a steel trap about to bite her in two. "Yes, well I apologize for that, Mr. McShane, but I have a job to do, and I can't allow friendship to get in the way."

"Apparently."

The moment his fingers touched the tips of her lacy white gloves, he swore he could feel a spark of something that didn't bode well for friendship. Allowing the briefest of handshakes, she quickly jerked away as if bitten by a snake, eyes averted while she swiftly took her seat. "Where's Miss Willoughby?" she asked, fingers shaking when she removed her notes from the portfolio, methodically shuffling them into a perfect, little stack.

"Running late." The tic in his cheek competed with the twitch of his lips, her nervousness taming some of his anger over the infuriating article she wrote. *Good.* She needed to be nervous around him because he sure in the devil was nervous around her. His every nerve and emotion was tied up in knots over the upset she stirred. The angst. The frustration. The loss of self-control.

The attraction.

Stomach growling, he sat back down, pretty sure a full stomach was needed to form any viable truce, but he'd do his best to get the job done, then get out of town. "Said she wanted to go over budgets with the mayor before our meeting," he said in a curt tone, taking a cue from the woman across from him by avoiding her gaze. "Wants us to forge on without her as it could take a while."

And "forge on" they did, although "fight on" might be more apt, given the roadblocks Finn encountered the first hour the woman almost jabbered nonstop.

"No man is going to take off his hat, gun, or spurs, Miss Bell, so you may as well ask him to come naked." He kneaded the bridge of his nose, wondering if the men of Virginia City had any idea the grief he was taking on their behalf.

She bent in over the table as if to stress both her points *and* him. "No woman wants to dance with a man armed with a gun that could go off or spurs that could rip her dress. And everyone knows it's pure courtesy for a gentleman to remove his hat indoors."

"It's a blasted barn," he shouted, "with daylight shining through more cracks in the wall than the doors and windows." His jaw started to grind. "Hats and guns stay, but I'll give you the spurs."

Her eyes narrowed as if that were exactly what she wanted to do—give him a few spurs. "No guns, no spurs," she said in a sweet voice underlaid with pure iron, "and I'll concede on the hats with a civil suggestion at the door that they be removed."

His lips gummed together. Boy, he'd like to "remove" a few things himself right about now, and it sure wasn't his hat.

The prattle continued until she struck another nerve. "And no tobacco, spittoons, or alcohol will be allowed indoors at the gala," she stated with a now-familiar flourish of her pen as she recorded all notes.

His jaw swung open, almost unhinged. "For the hundredth time, it's outside in a bloomin' barn, Miss Bell, not some high-falutin' ballroom in Manhattan. Men chew tobacco here," he articulated loud and clear, "and for the love of sanity, this town was practically built on saloons."

Her smile was polite, but the steel in her jaw was not. "It's one dance, Mr. McShane. It won't kill them to abstain in the name of civility. And no lady wants to dance with a gentleman—and I use the term loosely—who reeks of spirits and tobacco."

"You're only going to drive them to drink a whole lot more beforehand," he said, craving a drink himself right about now, "guaranteeing lots of sloppy drunks on your silly puncheon dance floor."

"No tobacco, no alcohol," she emphasized, then babbled on until the next twist of his arm a few moments later.

"I'm telling you flat-out, Liberty, you can't have a string quartet at a hoedown—it's a doggone barn dance, not a concert hall." His patience as thin as the strings in that blasted quartet, he glared across the table. Okay, all right, he was willing to concede on bows of bunting till he was red, white, and blue in the face. He even agreed to her ridiculous request to build a rough-hewn log dance floor for the Poppys' rickety barn, but blue blazes, enough was enough!

"It's an anniversary gala, Mr. McShane," she said carefully, far more patient than he, "and for a city known as the 'richest city in America,' we are also one of the most cosmopolitan places in the world. I hardly think a banjo and a washboard have the character to make a favorable impression on the many government officials and dignitaries sure to attend."

"Horse biscuits!" He launched to his feet and loomed in to go eye-to-eye, knuckles white as he leaned on the table. "News flash, Miss Bell, this is not New York City with its fancy airs and lardy-dardy ways. This is Virginia City, built on the backs of miners who chew, spit, and swear, and I guarantee if we hire strings, they'll be stringing *me* up for defamation of *their* character."

She shot up faster than one of those Roman candles they always set off on the Fourth of July, with just as many sparks in her eyes. "Oh, now, *there's* a valid reason to do things my way. Just because you lack culture, Mr. McShane, is no reason to deny others the chance to move forward."

"You want to move forward?" He slammed his fist on the table in lieu of wringing her pretty neck. "Then stop butting me at every turn so we can get something done."

She matched him with a thump on the table and raised him a brow. "You want something done? Then go back to your barn and take a nap in the hay, while somebody with a little vision leads the way."

That was the last straw—the one that obviously came from the barn where he napped. He rose to his full height with a tic in his jaw. "Fiddles and banjos," he said through clenched teeth, "no violins."

"One fiddle, one banjo, a cello, two violins, and a harp." Her gaze challenged him, along with the blasted press of those enticing pink lips.

He bit out the words like he was biting his tongue. "*One* violin. One banjo. One fiddle. One harmonica. No cello. No harp."

"No harp, no harmonica." She stared him down, defying him to counter.

He gave up the ghost, no energy left to deal with a woman who both intrigued and incited. "Fine," he said with a press of his temples, wondering what was louder—the growl of his stomach or the headache pounding in his brain. "I'm going home."

"No!" She darted around the table, palm out to stop his departure. "We have too much to discuss. You can't possibly leave yet."

Fire licked the edge of the temper he'd forgotten he had. Liberty O'Shea may tell him what instruments would play at the dance and what he or the men were or were not going to do, but she was *not* going to tell him he couldn't go home. He grabbed his satchel and started for the door.

She blocked his way, hands stretched wide as if silk-clad arms could possibly deter him. "You are not going home, Griffin McShane, until we discuss every detail on my list, is that clear?"

No, but the twitch in his jaw was more than apparent. "I think you're perfectly capable of discussing everything on your own because heaven knows I've barely gotten a word in edgewise as it is, either with suggestions or decisions."

She caught her breath, mouth slacking open in shock. "Are you implying that I've monopolized this meeting tonight?"

He slacked a hip, his hunger and fatigue siphoning out every bit of manners his mama ever taught him. "No, Miss Bell, I'm not implying that at all. I'm saying it outright. You're bossy, pushy, and you like the sound of your own voice, so I'm going home where I can get some peace and quiet."

"Well, I never!"

"No, I don't suppose you have," he said, thinking the woman would be even more drop-dead pretty if she didn't talk so dad-burned much. "Because I'm sure those milksop dandies you're used to dealing with in New York toe the line. But this is Virginia City, Liberty Bell, and I'm a man who doesn't take kindly to a pushy woman. Good night."

"Oh, no you don't!" She sprinted to the door and slammed it closed, plastering her body in front with arms outstretched and palms to the door. "There are at least ten points left on my list to cover, mister, and I am not leaving until we're done."

"Oh, we're done, *Miss* O'Shea," he ground out, the rare usage of her real surname an indication that his usual tease and banter was as empty as his stomach. "Now get out of my way."

"No." She responded with that same determined glint in her eyes she'd always had in spelling bees and science fairs, triggering a hair of his humor—but only a hair. She braced her arms in a tight fold, and he swore the low heels of her green satin ankle boots—which matched her expensive dress to a toe—would leave dents in the polished hardwood floor. The almond-shaped eyes snapped with green fire, igniting both his temper and something far more dangerous to them both. She gave him a sassy jut of her chin. "We can finish our meeting here or at the table, Mr. McShane, your choice."

"Oh, so now I have a choice?" His brows shot high in mockery, mostly to head off a twitch of a smile. They slashed low again as his voice ground to a growl. "No, ma'am, I'm tired of your yammering and I mean to go home. So I'm not going to tell you again, Liberty Bell— move that fancy dress of yours out of my way, or I'm going to move it for you."

"You wouldn't!" Those full pink lips parted in shock, and he mentally tasted them in his mind, grazing their softness with his mouth.

"Try me." He singed her with a glare as hot as the fire she'd lit in his belly.

She studied him in blessed silence for several moments,

as if gauging the validity of his threat, probably not even aware she was biting that lush lower lip he ached to lay claim to. And then the bodice of that incredible dress rose and fell as she switched tracks as smoothly as the V&T, appearing to take a different tact. "Finn, please," she said in a soft voice that would have melted his insides if he trusted her. Which he didn't. "Just twenty minutes more, and our meeting will be over, I promise."

He stood his ground, eyes fixed on emerald eyes fringed with thick lashes instead of those deadly pink lips. Liberty O'Shea had an awful lot to learn about him if she thought she could get anywhere with feminine wiles, which galled him even more than a pushy woman. Didn't work with Jo Beth, and it sure in the devil wasn't going to work with the woman who'd just dragged him through the mud in the biggest newspaper in town. At least pushy women were honest—right out there with their bossy demands rather than hiding an agenda to control or manipulate. Besides, the day he'd let Liberty O'Shea win an argument was the day he'd pack up and leave town. And he wasn't going anywhere.

Except home.

"Hate to break it to you, Miss Bell, but our meeting is over. *Now.*" Tucking his satchel under his arm, he looped both hands around that tiny, little waist and hiked her up in the air so fast, all he heard was the catch of her breath. Without ceremony, he plopped her down behind him, battling a grin when she squealed and wobbled like a newborn calf on mother's milk with rum. Snatching his hat off the hook, he slapped it on his head and opened the door. "Good night, Miss Bell. See you next week."

Slam! The door banged closed with a stiff breeze, almost taking his nose with it while a wild-eyed firecracker bonded herself to the door. "You *are* going to listen to me, you mule-brained skunk, if I have to nail this door shut and your shoes to the floor!"

Finn blinked, not sure whether to laugh or cry. He'd always heard redheads had volatile tempers, but he'd honestly had no idea. Although Liberty had never been what you called mild-mannered in school and certainly testier than most girls he knew, she'd never lost control like this before. It was almost like this was her own personal vendetta against the dominance of men in a society that knew little else. A battle of wills she obviously intended to win, but he had some bad news for the little spitfire.

He intended to win too.

In more ways than one.

Sparks and words were flying, but all he could do was glare, the fire in his belly slowly smoldering out of control when his gaze flicked to her lips and held. That perfectly beautiful mouth was just a yapping away, but the only thing he heard was the violent thud of his own pulse and the sound of those lips calling him home ...

"And another thing, Finn McShane," she said, slapping her hands to her hips, "if you don't march right back to that table and pull your load, I will not only tell the mayor, but I will tell Miss Willoughby and Mrs. Poppy as well."

Her words suddenly registered, and he could do nothing but shake his head, shades of the old Liberty tattling to their teachers coming to mind. He grinned while he mauled the back of his neck, pretty sure he'd never meet another woman who could fire up every emotion in his body quite like her. "You know, Liberty, you may have grown up into a woman with a fancy degree, but deep down you're still that spoiled little brat who just wants to get her own way." He slacked a hip and folded his arms, shuttered eyes issuing one more warning. "Now we can try this all over again next week if you're willing to behave, but I'm going home, and I suggest you do the same. Now please move."

"Or what?" She locked her arms to her chest like him and angled a brow, apparently under the mistaken notion she had the upper hand. "You going to manhandle me again, you big bully? Well, there's nothing you can do to get me to move except sit back down and act like a civil human being."

"Ha! As if you would even know what that is." He blasted out a sigh and dropped his head, hands perched low on his hips. "Okay, lady, I'm going to ask you one more time, real nice and civil-like ..." He peered up beneath hooded eyes, a near smile on his face. "Will you please move out of my way?"

"Nope." She smiled and shook her head, as if quite confident he was on the thaw. She clutched her hands behind her back like a little girl about to misbehave, green eyes issuing a dare. "And you can't make me."

He sighed. *Poor, misguided, little rich girl.* "Yeah?" He pushed the brim of his hat up. "Watch me." Hurling his satchel to the floor, he heard the catch of her breath when he struck like lightning with an arm to her waist. Jerking her close, he kissed the daylights out of her while her boots dangled in the air. Unfortunately, the moment he tasted those soft lips parted in surprise, he was struck by a little lightning of her own, electrifying every nerve in his body while his blood simmered to a dangerous boil.

When a telltale mew escaped her throat, he was helpless to contain the low moan that rose deep in his belly. Butting her to the door, he cradled her face in his hands, longing pumping through his veins as he claimed the sweetest lips he'd ever known—and he'd known plenty—completely disarmed by the scent of her skin, the soft flesh of her ear. Sure, he'd dreamed of kissing Liberty O'Shea for as long as he could remember, but he never expected this—a kiss that could surely tame his taste for all other women.

The very thought bucked like a thorn-saddled bull, and with a rush of icy mountain water surging through his veins, he dropped her to the floor like he'd been bit by a rattler. She teetered precariously—along with his heart—eyes glazed and mouth still open in shock. Mustering all the calm he owned—which was a mite low at the moment—he yanked his hat down low and reached for the knob. She bolted away like he was a grizzly fresh up from a nap, and Finn had to stifle a chuckle, tossing her a wink as he opened the door. "Told you."

He startled at the sight of Miss Willoughby hurrying down the hall, papers fluttering in her hand while heat seared his collar. "Oh, Finn, I truly apologize for the delay, but the mayor was in one of his chattier moods." Her pace slowed as her eyes flicked from his sheepish grin to Liberty's pale face, a crimp of concern creasing her brow. "Is everything all right?"

"Oh, yes, ma'am, we're all done here and on our way home."

Relief washed over the schoolteacher's face as she unleashed a grateful sigh. "Oh, good! I was so worried, but it sounds like you two made some good progress."

Tipping his hat, he couldn't resist a smirk over his shoulder, deflecting the wild beat of his pulse with a leisurely wink. "Yes, ma'am, I believe we did."

CHAPTER TEN

"IF IT TAKES EVERY BREATH in my body, he is *not* going to win!" Liberty glared across the Poppys' rolling meadow where Finn McShane wielded a hammer on behalf of the ladies of The Brass Rail Saloon. Her eyes narrowed as she watched the girls fawn all over him and Milo while the two men built the saloon façade they volunteered to make for the Brass Rail's booth. Their laughter echoed in the valley, making Libby wish she had whacked that insufferable rogue silly the moment he'd kissed her in City Hall.

Watching him out of the corner of her eye, she slapped red paint on the side of her schoolhouse booth with way too much force. And she would have whacked him, too, if he hadn't shocked the everliving sense out of her. Making her too stunned to move. Too breathless to speak.

Too attracted to stop.

The vile memory accosted her all over again, causing her pulse to sprint and her cheeks to burn. She smacked the side of the booth Kitty's brother had built for them, splattering red paint all over her work dress. "Honestly, I don't know what the women of this town see in him—he's nothing but a cocky womanizer."

Kitty's low chuckle did nothing for the heat in Libby's face. "Come on, Libs, if you can't see what the women in this town see in Griffin McShane, I suggest you have Dr. Thompson fit you for spectacles." She paused on the other side of the booth with a red-soaked paintbrush in hand, chest expanding with an appreciative sigh. "Rumor has it that Finn's kisses can melt a girl into a puddle." She shot Libby a wink. "At least according to Jo Beth."

Okay, Libby was pretty sure her face now matched the side of her booth. She commenced to fanning herself with her paintbrush, flicking paint specks all over the ground and herself. "That's because he's probably kissed every female in the blessed county," she muttered, wishing she could blame her shallow breathing on the muggy day.

"*Welllll* ... he sure hasn't kissed me," Kitty said with a cagey smile, her gaze darting to the back of the booth where Martha was just finishing up with white trim. "How 'bout you, Martha? Has Finn ever kissed you?"

Libby was grateful when her notoriously shy friend turned the exact shade of the booth, deflecting some of the warmth Libby felt in her own face. "Merciful heavens no!" Her freckles suddenly bleached near white as the paint on her brush. "Makes me plumb dizzy just thinking about it."

Kitty homed in on Libby, the twinkle in her friend's eyes assuring her she was up to no good. "So ... what about you, Libs?" She waggled her brows. "Has Finn ever kissed you?"

Heatstroke claimed her on the spot, much as Finn had two weeks before, scorching her body—and her memories—all over again.

"I knew it!" Kitty brandished her brush like a threat, the gleam in her eyes not boding well for the awful secret Libby worked so hard to hide. "*That's* why you begged Martha and me to go to the last two planning meetings with you, isn't it? And *that's* why you've been as skittish as a doe whenever the man even looks your way. I swear you turn seven shades of red if he teases you instead of cutting him down to size like you used to in school."

Kitty set her brush across the bucket of paint sitting

on the ground and faced Libby head-on, hands on her hips. "Liberty O'Shea, I have been your best friend since you moved to Virginia City, and you have never kept a secret from me before, so I want to know right now ..." She dipped her head to peer into Liberty's downcast eyes, obviously softening her tone when she saw a glaze of tears. "Did Finn McShane kiss you?"

Libby's lashes flickered closed, the recurring thought of Finn's lips on hers branding her for life.

"Oh my stars, he *did*, didn't he!"

Libby's lids slowly lifted to face the music, staring at Kitty as if she were in a daze while Martha scrambled over to join them, the whites of her eyes spanning wider than Kitty's.

"Liberty O'Shea!" Kitty demanded with a stamp of her foot, "why didn't you tell us that Finn McShane kissed you?"

Kitty's volume jolted Liberty out of her trance, heart slamming against her ribs as her gaze darted around to see if anybody had heard. "Kitty Faye Jones, hush!" Liberty rasped, cheeks flaming all the more when she caught Finn glancing their way. "Sweet mother of pearl, why don't you just announce it from the bandstand?"

Huffing out a noisy blast of air, Kitty dragged Liberty behind their booth and pinned her with two paint-stained hands as she gave her a little shake. "I can't believe you didn't tell us!" she whispered loudly, clearly peeved to have been denied the juiciest morsel of news in their young lives. "When on earth did it happen and for heaven's sake, *how?* And most importantly ..." Kitty's lips squirmed into a wicked smile. "How was it?"

Liberty was certain the blood in her cheeks had crawled clear up to her bangs, a perfect match for her auburn hair. She put a hand to her eyes, still embarrassed over the whole sordid scene.

The same sordid scene she dreamed about every single night.

"It happened at the second planning meeting a few weeks ago," she whispered, the very memory even making her hands sweat. "When Miss Willoughby ran late and Finn was being a stubborn mule about every little thing."

"And we both know he was the only one, right?" Kitty and Martha giggled in unison, prompting Liberty to lift her hand from her eyes and give them a glare.

Ignoring Kitty's comment, she continued on. "The next thing I know, he jumps up and charges to the door like one of Mr. Wilson's prize bulls, and I had to fight fire with fire, didn't I? So I blocked the door, refusing to let him leave till we finished the meeting."

"Of course you did," Kitty said with a grin, "until he kissed the fire right out of you, suddenly making you meek as a lamb whenever he's around."

"Horse puddles!" Liberty hissed, occupying herself with flicking paint specks on the grass while her lips jabbed into a scowl. "I just refuse to waste anymore breath on that mule of a man than necessary because he doesn't listen anyway," she said with a glower in said mule's direction. She attempted to sidetrack the inquisition with a sudden keen interest in their booth, squinting as she circled to assess. "Just a little more paint, I think, and we should be done, ready to mount the school bell."

"Ohhhh nooooo you don't!" Kitty jerked her back with a hook of her arm, brows arched high in question, along with Martha's. "You still haven't told us—how was it?" she breathed.

There was *no* way Liberty would ever admit just *how* much Finn's kiss had affected her. Mercy, she could barely admit it to herself! Determined to sidestep further curiosity—and the awful truth of the situation—she marched right back over to her side of the booth with a firm press of lips, slapping more paint on with a vengeance. "Awful! I have no earthly idea what Jo Beth or any girl in this town sees in Griffin McShane. Frankly, the man leaves me cold," she fibbed, fingers crossed and carefully hidden in the folds of her splattered work dress.

"Cold." Kitty crossed her arms with a suspicious dip of brows, her tone reflecting more disbelief than query.

"Yes, 'cold,'" Liberty repeated with an extra thwack of the brush. "Icier than snowcaps in a Nevada blizzard, if you must know. Pert near shivered the rest of the night." She swallowed hard.

Not exactly a lie ...

Kitty chuckled. "I'll bet you're not the only one shivering, not with that 'cold' shoulder you've been giving him the last few weeks."

"*Which* I fully intend to continue," Liberty said, putting on the finishing touch before stepping back to study it with a critical eye. "Until the man turns blue with frostbite."

"*Brrrr,*" Kitty said with a teasing chatter of teeth, wiping her brush with a rag. "So between his frostbite and your cold shoulder, maybe Martha and I need to wear coats and gloves to the next meeting. You know, just to stay warm?"

Unable to thwart a grin, Liberty shook her head, repacking their painting supplies in the wood wagon she'd had since she was a small girl. "No need, ladies, because although the man leaves me cold, his bull-headed personality always manages to keep my temper warm, so I assure you, there will be more than enough heat."

"Well, I'm certainly counting on that," Kitty said with a wink, "because what's a Fourth of July planning committee without a few sparks?"

Libby cut loose with a grunt. "I can promise you right now there will be *no* sparks, my friend, because I refuse to let that man rile me anymore than he already has."

"An easy enough promise to keep if Martha and I are around," Kitty said with a sly smile, "but what about when the two of you are alone?"

An involuntary shiver skated Libby's spine, which she

quickly deflected with a bold thrust of her chin. "We won't be—*ever* again, not if I can help it."

"But what if you can't?" Martha worried her lip. "I mean, there are bound to be times when Kitty and I won't be there, Libs, so what are you going to do?"

"Ruffle his feathers, no doubt, till he kisses her again." Kitty grinned.

"Absolutely not!" Libby said with complete conviction. "The day I allow myself to be alone with that rogue ever again will be the day I ride Bessie backwards down the middle of Main Street." She snatched the handle of the wagon with a confident smile, determination squaring her shoulders while she gave them a wink. "*In* my bloomers."

"Hey, Liberty Bell, wait up!"

The sound of the rogue's voice caused a low groan to leak through Libby's lips along with all of her bravado.

Finn loped across the field in his typical easy manner, shirt unbuttoned and flapping in the breeze. Slowing, he stopped in front of Liberty, muscles slick with sweat as he lifted his hat to wipe his damp brow with the rolled-up sleeve of his shirt. "Forgot to tell you Mrs. Poppy invited us to dinner tomorrow night to discuss the layout and final setup of the barn."

Liberty stared, mouth hanging open, allowing only one hoarse word to escape. "*Us?*"

A bead of sweat trickled down his neck onto a bronzed chest lightly sprinkled with hair, producing some sweat of her own on the palms of her hands. "Yes, 'us,' Liberty Bell—you and me," he said with a patient smile, "because we're the committee co-chairs, remember?"

Sweet angel of mercy, as if I could forget!

"We're supposed to be there by six, so I'll pick you up at 5:30."

"*No!* I mean … I'd rather meet you there, if you don't mind," she said in a rush, heart hammering in her chest. "I prefer to walk."

"Suit yourself," he said in a slow drawl. His eyes never strayed from hers as he slowly buttoned his shirt with that maddening half smile that told her he knew exactly how nervous she was. "But I insist on escorting you home, because I may be a 'mule-brained skunk,'" he said with a lazy tip of his hat, "but I'm a skunk with manners." He turned and strolled back to his bevy of admirers without a glance back, and all Libby could do was stare, all blood effectively drained from her face.

"Come on, Libs," Kitty said with a loop of Libby's arm while Martha took over the wagon, "you don't look so good, sweetie, so let's get you home."

"What on earth am I going to do?" Her whisper was little more than a croak as she allowed her friends to lead her away, mind as numb as her body.

Towing the wagon, Martha offered a look of sympathy over her shoulder as Kitty hooked a supportive arm to Libby's waist. "The only thing you can do, Libs," Kitty said with a gentle squeeze, the sympathy in her tone unable to mask a tinge of a tease. She winked. "Saddle up Bessie."

CHAPTER ELEVEN

" **S**O, GRIFFIN—HOW IS THE FESTIVAL planning coming along?"

Finn glanced up from his third piece of cherry pie, pretty sure a cherry pit just lodged in his throat. Up till now, the dinner at the Poppys' had been nothing but pleasant. The mouthwatering smell of cherry pie still warm from the oven lingered in the air, complemented by equally warm conversation with the two people he admired most in the world. A summer breeze tickled eyelet curtains, ushering in the cool of evening along with the scent of honeysuckle in a cozy kitchen where he'd enjoyed sustenance over the years, spiritual and otherwise. Sensing a sudden stiffness in Liberty as she sipped tea across the table, he grabbed his own cup and quickly downed it, clearing his throat with a polite smile. "Just fine and dandy, Mrs. Poppy, right on schedule and smooth as silk."

The planning, that is. The relationship with his co-chair? He wolfed down the rest of his pie in one massive gulp. *More like burlap rolled in cockleburs.*

"Good, good. And, Liberty dear—do you agree?" Mrs. Poppy cocked her head in question, tilting her trademark donut bun of silvery-white hair more cockeyed than usual. Practically a grandmother to Finn, the elderly woman calmly drank her tea, offering a secret smile that matched a suspicious sparkle in her blue eyes.

Liberty's head shot up, as skittish as a prairie dog in a barrel of bobcats. Her gaze met Finn's, and he took satisfaction in the blush that stained her cheeks, reminding him how pretty she was when she wasn't yammering to get her own way. A lump bobbed in that creamy throat of hers that had always reminded him of a stately swan. Chewing on the edge of a nervous smile, her teeth tugged on those lush lips like Finn so longed to do. "Uh, yes, Mrs. Poppy, it appears Mr. McShane and I have everything under control."

Except our feelings for each other, Finn mused with a familiar hint of regret, studying Liberty as she launched into a thorough overview of everything they'd accomplished so far. Watching her now—her face flushed with excitement and eyes aglow with passion over the subject at hand—Finn couldn't help but wish some of that powerful passion could be directed his way. He'd always been attracted to her, of course—something he took great pains to hide—but over the last month of working with her so closely, he'd gained a new respect that only deepened the draw. Beneath that fire-red hair and trigger temper beat a heart of compassion for others, a do-or-die allegiance to the underdog, something Finn felt strongly about too. Which only reinforced the attraction.

True, her overly vocal obsession with women's rights had riled him at first, but when he learned his mother's cousin lost her family's home to "a no-good deserter of a husband," he quickly changed his mind. The low-down skunk had returned to sell the house right out from under the poor woman, leaving her and her children out on the streets. That sort of travesty could have happened to his mother and him as well, he realized, based on the lack of property rights for women. Suddenly Finn saw Liberty's "dad-burned cockamamie goals" in a whole new light—along with the woman who held them. The very woman who had never, *ever* been attracted to him and made no bones about it.

Until "the kiss."

A slow smile eased across his lips. From that moment on, he'd noticed a definite skittishness in her whenever he was around, almost as if that one kiss had tamed the spitfire in her, at least where he was concerned. Since then, she'd been almost demure, guarded, armed with the protection of her two best friends to make sure he didn't get too close. His mouth tamped into a tight line. And doggone-it, he *wanted* to get close! To sample once again the sweet taste of lips that had ruined him for other women, reveling in the passion and fire that had always drawn him like a moth to flame.

A hint of melancholy eased his facial muscles as he absently fiddled with the fork on his plate. An old codger from his days on the transcontinental railroad once told him male moths dive into a candle flame because they think it's a female looking for a mate, but they just end up fried to a crisp. Finn's mouth took a slant. He certainly could attest to that. The very fire and fervor that kindled this hopeless attraction to Liberty O'Shea was the same fire and fervor that singed him every time he got too close.

His gaze flicked up to take in how her auburn hair gleamed in the lamplight. Or how the musical sound of her laughter filled the Poppys' intimate kitchen with a contentment sweeter than Mrs. Poppy's pie. Against his will, a fierce longing curled in his chest. He'd always suspected his affection for Liberty went deeper than just the race of his pulse. But it wasn't until she walked into his office that fateful day that he realized for him, the attraction was so much more. Stubborn and hot-headed to a fault, she was also more passionate and exciting than any woman he'd ever known, and completely devoted to the common good, no matter the cost. To him, she was the essence of true "liberty"—beautiful and bright, wild and free, infusing her heart and soul into everything she loved.

And sweet mother of mercy, how he wished that were him!

He unleashed a silent sigh while Mrs. Poppy peppered Liberty with questions, his thoughts trailing to the improbability of he and Liberty ever falling in love. In her eyes, he'd always be nothing more than salt in her wound, a cocky womanizer who'd been the bane of her existence. And he supposed that'd been true at one time, before Pastor and Mrs. Poppy had gotten a hold of him and taught him about true faith. Since then, no matter how many ladies he'd squired about town, other than kisses, he'd followed the straight and narrow. As difficult as it had been, he'd learned to steer clear of his former carnal nature when it came to women and focus more on his land.

Until that blasted kiss changed it all ...

"So, Liberty," Mrs. Poppy said as she poured more tea, a definite smile in her tone, "how are you and Griffin getting along? Still fighting like cats and dogs?"

Liberty's face leeched as white as the cream she'd just poured into her tea, gaze skittering from Mrs. Poppy to Finn and back. "Uh, just fine, ma'am," she lied through her teeth, smile as stiff as the spoon she stirred in her cup.

"Excellent!" Mrs. Poppy returned the tea kettle to the stove and sat back down, gaze twinkling as much as the dimples in her moon cheeks. "I think you and Griffin make such a lovely pair, dear, that I'm delighted you're partnering as co-chairs for our committee. After all, who knows?" She took a sip of her tea, humor dancing in her eyes over the rim of her cup. "Maybe it will evolve into a partnership of a more permanent nature."

Finn bit back a smile when Liberty started to hack, her china cup rattling back to its saucer in a messy slosh of tea before she pressed a napkin to her mouth.

Mrs. Poppy commenced to slapping Liberty's back. "Goodness, dear, are you all right?"

The scrape of Pastor Poppy's chair proved to be a timely interruption. "Now, Clara, the young woman *will be* if you stop prying into her personal life, playing matchmaker again." He pushed in his chair and carried his plate to the sink. "Finn, now that I'm fat as a tick, how 'bout we walk some of Mrs. Poppy's fine food off with a trip to the barn to work on the layout?"

"Yes, sir," Finn said, standing to push in his own chair. "After a meal like that and three pieces of pie, I'd say that's a given."

Liberty jumped up so quickly, her chair rattled. She immediately began collecting dirty dishes and utensils, completely focused on the task at hand. "Let me do the dishes, Mrs. Poppy, please," she said, clearly avoiding Finn's gaze. "You three head on over to the barn, and I'll join you as soon as I can."

Mrs. Poppy chuckled as she toddled to the sink, dumping dessert plates into a washtub. She set her teakettle on the far side of the cookstove to slowly warm the dishwater while she tossed an impish look over her shoulder. "Oh heavens, no! Goodness—you and Finn are the heart and soul of this fair, young lady, so your input is absolutely critical. Besides," she said, snatching a broom from her pantry, "I'll have plenty of time to clean up after you two leave, so let's just mosey on over to the barn right now and get to work." She hooked an arm through Liberty's to lead her out the back screen door while Finn and Pastor Poppy followed.

Liberty screeched to a stop on the back porch, cheeks as pink as some of the tea roses blooming in Mrs. Poppy's garden. "Uh, I think perhaps I should excuse myself to use the necessary first, ma'am, but I'll join you as soon as I can, all right?" Slipping from the woman's hold, she darted down the steps and practically sprinted to the Poppys' outhouse at the far edge of the yard.

"Goodness, I hope she's not feeling poorly," Mrs. Poppy said with a pinch of brows, allowing Finn to usher her down the steps. "That would be awful if my dinner gave her indigestion."

Mr. Poppy's chuckle drifted on summer air perfumed by roses and honeysuckle from his wife's renowned garden. "I can assure you, my dear, if that poor girl does have indigestion, it wasn't the dinner that caused it."

Finn laughed, so very grateful for these two people who had sown so much love and faith into his life. Breathing in the heady scents of Mrs. Poppy's garden, he silently thanked God for providing such strong spiritual mentors. Their love and support bloomed as rich and lush as the riot of color and scents from the garden that surrounded their charming house.

Famous for poppies cultivated from seeds Pastor Poppy brought back from a missionary trip to Asia, the garden was an exotic rainbow of poppies, roses, lavender, and other perennials and herbs. Nearing the peak of their bloom, the poppies offered a loose and lush look to the backyard in varying shades of white, pink, mauve, lavender, and maroon. To Finn, it was a feast for the senses with the heavenly merge of the faint hint of roses, pine, honeysuckle, and mint.

"Your garden is lovely as usual, Mrs. Poppy," Finn said with true appreciation, "with what appears to be a bumper crop of poppies this year."

Her little-girl giggle drifted in the perfumed air as he ushered her toward the barn, which thanks to Pastor Poppy's faithful congregation, was one of the largest in the area. "Oh my, yes," she said with a proud gleam in her eyes, "plenty of poppy seeds for my award-winning cake." She halted and turned to face Finn dead-on, her smiling eyes suddenly narrowing the slightest bit. "But enough about *my* garden, Griffin McShane. I'm more interested in *yours* right now, young man."

Finn blinked. "Pardon me?"

"Your garden, Finn," she whispered, peeking over her shoulder as if to make sure Liberty wasn't anywhere around. "Where I suspect your feelings for Liberty are sprouting faster than Jack's beanstalk in the sky."

Finn's mouth plunked open in shock.

"And don't you dare deny you have feelings for that young woman, Griffin McShane, because it's as plain as the nose on your face."

"It is?" Finn slapped a hand to his nose, shocked that anyone could read him that easily when it came to Liberty. His mouth went flat. But then Milo had, so why should it be any surprise that the town's notorious matchmaker had homed in on his secret, especially a woman who was more like blood?

"Yes, it is, young man, and frankly, I want to know what you plan to do about it?"

Cuffing the back of his neck, Finn kicked at a clump in the dirt, suddenly feeling more like fifteen than twenty-five. "Aw, Mrs. Poppy, Liberty and I just flat-out don't get along. That woman is a flame to my fuse, so it's never long before one of us gets burned."

Raising a finger, Mrs. Poppy leaned in with a no-nonsense squint that always made him sweat. "Fire is a precious commodity, young man, and don't you forget it. Handle it carefully, and it will keep you warm for the rest of your life." She shot another glance behind her before peering up with a probing glare, wagging that chunky finger in his face like a gun. "I've had this sixth sense about you and Liberty O'Shea ever since she pushed you in the pond out back for calling her ugly. But you didn't really think that, did you?"

Heat blasted Finn's face as he stared at his boots. "No, ma'am, I guess I didn't, but she was just so much fun to rile." He looked up with a crooked grin. "A real spitfire, you know?"

Pastor Poppy chuckled. "Yes, son, I surely do, because that's exactly how my Clara was before the Lord opened my eyes to the most exciting and wonderful woman I ever met."

Hooking his thumbs in the pockets of his denim dunga-
rees, Finn shrugged his shoulders with a melancholy smile.
"I wish I could say that was the case with Liberty and me,
but the woman outright despises me, sir."

Pastor Poppy scratched his ear, head cocked as he studied Finn closely. "Have you prayed about it, son? Because
I would have missed the greatest joy I've ever known if I
hadn't prayed for God's wisdom and direction." He paused,
eyes in a squint. "And something tells me it's the same for
you. I've watched the two of you grow up over the years,
and seems to me there's always been this spark between
you, just like Clara says."

Finn shook his head, body tingling at the very thought.
"Oh, there's way more than a spark, sir," he said with a
chuckle, "but I just worry there's too much friction for a
truly meaningful relationship, you know?"

Pastor Poppy hooked an arm to his wife's waist. "Been
my experience, Finn, that friction is what sets two hearts
afire, like me and my Clara, isn't that right, darlin'?"

"Oh my stars, yes," Mrs. Poppy said with a comical roll of
eyes. "Goodness, the pastor and I butted heads so often, it's
a wonder neither of us got a concussion, although we did
give each other plenty of headaches before we fell in love."

Finn laughed and shook his head. "Yes, ma'am, Libby
and I have certainly given each other our fair share, that's
for sure. But if I thought for one split hair of a second that
Liberty and I could end up like you and Pastor Poppy, I
would surely brave the flames of that woman's wrath, I can
tell you that."

"Well, do me a favor then, son," the pastor said with a slap
of Finn's shoulder. "Ask the Good Lord for His opinion,
why don't you, then just follow the peace. Better a headache than a heartache at missing out on what the Almighty
has in store. After all, you can always take willow bark for
that headache, my boy, but heartache stays with a body for
a long, long time." He took his wife's arm. "Come along,

my dear—we've got a barn to tidy up." Ushering his wife in, the two of them teased and chatted as they lit lanterns to stave off the darkness from the onset of dusk.

Watching them, Finn couldn't help but wonder if he and Liberty could possibly ever end up as happy as that. Squinting up at the rafters, he said that prayer Pastor Poppy suggested and instantly felt the tension in his body slowly leak out. Instead, it was replaced by a flicker of hope that burned as brightly as the Poppys' lanterns all over the barn, casting a soft glow over Finn's mood.

"Fire is a precious commodity, young man, and don't you forget it. Handle it carefully, and it will keep you warm for the rest of your life."

Finn grinned as he rolled up his sleeves, thinking there was nothing he'd rather do than "handle" that pretty stick of dynamite called Liberty O'Shea. His mouth tipped off-center. *As long as she keeps me warm, that is.* His thoughts sobered considerably.

Instead of blowing up in my face.

CHAPTER TWELVE

"**Y**OU AND GRIFFIN MAKE SUCH a lovely pair ..."
Liberty gulped for surely the hundredth time,
palms plastered to the inside of the outhouse door. Lean-
ing against it, she waited for the frantic clip of her heart
to subside. "Lovely pair, indeed," she muttered with an
unwelcome rush of warmth, the very idea giving her chills.
And not the cold kind.

Because the truth was, Finn wanted absolutely nothing
to do with her, and frankly, she'd felt exactly the same way.
Until that stupid kiss.

She wrinkled her nose, the sudden heat purling through
her as unwelcome as the rank odor of the privy. Chewing
on the edge of her lip, she wondered how long she could
hide out before someone came looking for her.

Tap. Tap. Tap. "Dear, are you all right?" The concern in
Mrs. Poppy's voice almost unleashed a groan of guilt from
the pit of Libby's stomach.

"Yes, ma'am, just a touch of indigestion, but I'm better
now," she said, unlatching the bolt before she swung the
door wide.

"Oh, I just knew it—my chili upset your stomach, didn't
it?"

No, not the chili ...

"Oh crumb! I should have started over when the silly
shaker lid for the red pepper fell into the pot." The old
woman's silver brows crinkled in concern. "Would you

like a bromide to settle your stomach?"

Liberty inhaled a hefty draw of fresh air, the heavenly scent of Mrs. Poppy's garden helping to calm her nerves. "No, ma'am, I'll be fine, truly." She slipped an arm through Mrs. Poppy's with a forced chuckle. "But I would like to get over to that barn before Co-chair McShane makes all the decisions."

The moment they entered the tall wooden structure, Liberty felt her tension melt away like the candles in the lanterns. The smell of hay and horse and leather reminded her just how much she'd loved riding and grooming her Palomino, Bessie, when she was younger.

"I'm afraid it's going to take some tidying up," Mrs. Poppy said with a rare crease in her forehead, "so we'll have to make sure we have lots of help when we set every-thing up."

Eyes wide, Liberty slowly circled in one spot, hands clasped to her chest in complete awe. Often utilized for church and civil functions due to its large size according to Finn, the Poppys' barn could almost be called "cozy." The pinks and purples of dusk peeked through various slats of the walls beneath a massive beamed roof that somehow felt so intimate. "Oh, Pastor and Mrs. Poppy," she whispered, "I'd forgotten how perfect this is! I was so busy building our booth last week, that I barely noticed when I ventured inside, but this is absolutely ideal for our dance!"

"Why thank you, my dear, we certainly hope so," the old woman said, hurrying over to light more lamps while Pastor Poppy dusted off an old table by the door with his broom. "And with the benches borrowed from church and the stage and dance floor you plan to build, I think this will not only make a lovely venue for the dance, but for the talent show too."

"Oh, it certainly will!" Liberty breathed in the sweet smell of hay while she flung her arms out and twirled, as if the packed mud floor were a dance floor in one of

New York's finest hotels. Clasping her hands in delight, she turned her attention to Finn, the affectionate look on his face putting a hitch in her pulse. "The carpentry volunteers are scheduled to begin building the stage tomorrow, correct, Mr. McShane?"

His light brown eyes softened to the color of warm caramel as a faint smile shadowed his lips. "It's Finn, Libby, remember?" he said, tossing a smile Mrs. Poppy's way as if to elicit her help in relaxing Liberty's reserved manner. "Formality seems so out of place in a barn, don't you think? Especially when two people are working closely together, week after week?"

"Absolutely," Mrs. Poppy piped up in no-nonsense assent. "For goodness' sake, Liberty, you've known Griffin since you two were battling in spelling bees, so there's no need for formality here, young lady."

"Yes, ma'am," Libby said with a quiet sigh, addressing Finn once again in a voice definitely shyer than before. "So our carpentry schedule begins tomorrow, Finn, is that correct? With completion slated for the last week of June?"

"Yes, Liberty, that's what we're shooting for." Offering a decidedly warmer smile, Finn proceeded to point out where he thought the stage should be built, walking out its length before asking Libby her opinion. Of course the two quibbled amicably over dance floor placement and size. But by the time they'd discussed additional hay-bale seating in the loft and dickered over placement of tables for the bakery contest, they were laughing and getting along like never before. The sun had long since set, filling the barn with cozy candlelight shadows and the music of crickets and frogs. So much so, in fact, that Liberty almost didn't want the evening to end.

Pastor Poppy peered up at the loft, eyes in a squint. "Finn, I'm not too sure how many bales of hay there are up there, so if you could check for me, I'd be much obliged."

"Oh, and while you're up there," Mrs. Poppy was quick

to add, "maybe you and Liberty can shift any bales close to the edge for seating so we have that all done?"

Finn grabbed a lantern and headed to the loft ladder. "Good idea," he said, slowly inching up with the lamp in hand. "But no need for Liberty to help, ma'am. That's second-cutting alfalfa we hauled up there as I recall, which is way too heavy for a girl."

"Says who?" Liberty stared up with hands on her hips, the glow of the evening fading a hair at the memory of high school battles, when Finn used to taunt her for being the weaker sex.

Finn paused to glance down, a smile twitching at the edge of his mouth. "Libby, trust me. Milo and I helped store these bales last year, so I know each and every one weighs pert near more than you—almost eighty pounds."

"Trust you?" Liberty mounted the first slat with a determined glint in her eye, a hint of jest gracing her tone. "You'll pardon me if that's a concept I'm not familiar with, *Finn*. But I assure you what I lack in strength, I will more than make up in grit and gumption."

"No doubt about that," Finn said with a shake of his head, smile notwithstanding.

Bracing her hands to the ladder, she carefully slipped a dainty boot to the first rung, a knot ducking in her throat before she haltingly tackled the second. "Because I don't know if you've noticed, Co-chairman Finn," she said in a voice as shaky as her legs, "but I'm not someone who shirks from a challenge."

Finn grinned. "No, ma'am, you're not," he said with a chuckle as he continued to mount the ladder.

She paused to watch on the second rung, completely mesmerized by broad shoulders that tapered into slim hips and a compact backside, an observation that toasted her cheeks hot when Finn caught her staring. Mortified, she quickly refocused on the rung before her, sucking in a deep draw of air before expelling it again in a raspy quiver.

"It's okay, you can do it," Finn said from above, not a trace of tease gilding his comment. "I promise you—there's nothing to be afraid of."

Liberty gulped as she took another tentative step, peeking up at the man who rattled her nerves more than the stupid ladder.

Wanna bet?

CHAPTER THIRTEEN

I *AM NOT AFRAID OF HEIGHTS. I am not afraid of heights.* Liberty halted halfway to fortify with more air, fingers pinched as white as her face, no doubt, from her death grip on the ladder.

"You don't have to do this, Libs." Finn's voice was soft, obviously for her ears alone as he crouched at the top. Apparently he was recalling his awful challenge to her his senior year to climb a tree during recess, paralyzing her until Miss Willoughby demanded he help her back down.

"Yes, I do," she whispered, more for herself than for him, the tender look in Finn's eyes doing nothing for her concentration. "I need to conquer my fear of heights once and for all."

And my fear of Finn McShane? A reedy breath seeped through her clenched teeth as she slowly crawled up, rung by tortuous rung.

Do broncs buck?

"Well, we best get busy with these two brooms, Pastor Poppy," Mrs. Poppy said. "If these youngsters can climb into that loft to do manual labor, I suppose the least you and I can do is start sweeping out this barn." She continued to chatter away down below, but Liberty could barely hear for the pounding of blood in her ears—both from her annoying fear of heights *and* the fact that Finn reached down to hook her waist, drawing her into the loft.

"Now, that wasn't so bad, was it?" he whispered in her

ear, both his arm and the warmth of his breath lingering far too long for comfort.

She swallowed hard. *No, not the climb* ...

The moment her feet touched solid flooring, she lurched away, almost losing her balance. In another hitch of her breath, he braced her tightly once more, the press of his body to hers doing far more damage than her fear. "It's okay, Libs," he said softly, rubbing her back with a gentleness that all but melted her on the spot. "Fear of heights is perfectly normal for most people, but I promise I would never let you fall ..."

Fall? She battled a gulp as he slowly released her, his heated gaze causing her heart to wobble more than her legs. *Oh, sweet mother of mercy—I think I already have!*

Finn hung the lantern on a nail and rolled his sleeves. "All righty, Miss O'Shea, let's push hay while the lantern shines," he quipped.

Hand to her chest to calm the traitorous thump of her heart, Liberty watched as he attacked a stack of bales taller than him, biceps bulging as he hefted several onto the floor. Following his lead, she bent to push one across the rough-hewn floor with an unexpected grunt, grateful she'd remembered to wear her work dress. "Oh my goodness," she huffed, taking a moment to catch her breath, "you weren't lying, Finn—these bales weigh a ton!"

He stopped mid-stride to jag a thick, dark brow. "I *never* lie, Miss O'Shea," he said in a husky tone, the two bales he carried obviously no hardship for a muscled body taut from clearing trees and chopping wood. "Or make a promise I can't keep."

Quickly averting her eyes, she attacked another bale, determined to focus more on working than on the man working beside her. After managing to shove a total of six bales to the front of the loft, she was no longer embarrassed over the grunts and groans it wracked from her body. But she and Finn enjoyed amiable conversation nonetheless while the mountain of hay slowly dwindled, even if hers was salted with breathless heaves.

"You know, sometimes I crave the smells of a barn," he said without the slightest exertion, a touch of wonder lacing his tone. Hands low on his hips, he assessed the remaining bales with a slow inhale. His chest expanded, as if with pride and pleasure over laboring in a barn. "I can't wait until I can build my own someday, being surrounded by so many things I love in one place: horses, hay, leather, oats." He shot her a crooked smile before hefting two more bales. "I guess that sounds silly to a girl."

"No, it doesn't at all." She tugged at another bale from the stack, carefully shimmying it forward till it toppled over. "I used to practically live in our barn grooming the horses, which was why it was one of my favorite places to be." Her tone turned wispy as she prodded more hay, remembering how free she always felt astride her palomino. "After riding the ridge, of course."

"I know, I used to see you," he said quietly, muscles straining as he carried more bales to the edge. "The prettiest red hair I ever did see, flowing behind you and shimmering in the sun. I remember thinking you were the most graceful and fluid rider I ever saw astride a horse."

"You did?" She paused, bent over a bale she was trying to scoot, his statement flushing her cheeks with a delicious warmth.

"I did." He pushed her bale the rest of the way to the edge with little or no effort, then led her over to sit. "You need a rest," he said, gently nudging her back down when she tried to get up. "We both do."

"Sounds like you two might be ready for some lemonade," Mrs. Poppy called, and both Finn and Liberty tossed a smile over their shoulders to the couple below.

"Sounds good, ma'am," Finn said, "but after we finish the last of these bales, though, which shouldn't take too long."

"Well, just come on in when you're ready, then, all right?"

"Yes, ma'am, will do." They watched as the Poppys departed arm in arm, then Finn popped a piece of hay between his teeth and straddled a bale. Eyes reflective, he studied her closely, the sudden intensity of his gaze leaving Liberty more breathless than lugging a loft full of hay. "Also thought you were the plum prettiest girl I ever did see, even at the scrawny age of twelve." A grin eased across his full lips while the piece of straw twirled in his mouth. "Of course I was pretty scrawny myself back then."

"I didn't think so," she said, avoiding his scrutiny to pluck some hay of her own, spinning it with her fingers. "You always seemed so much older and stronger than the rest of the boys."

"Oh, so you noticed." His chuckle braised her cheeks with more heat, and she looked away, reluctant to reconnect with those deadly hazel eyes that made her feel so nervous, so vulnerable.

So alive.

"I noticed," she said softly. She quickly bent to flick straw off her skirt, suddenly missing his former tease and taunts that had always stirred more ire than desire.

"Libby." The sound of her name on his tongue turned her insides to butter, and she closed her eyes as if somehow that might weaken the effect he had on her. But her pounding pulse and shallow breathing persisted, parching her mouth as dry as the piece of straw quivering in her hand.

He gently lifted her chin with his fingers, and a gasp parted from her lips when he caressed her jaw with the pad of his thumb. "And *I* noticed too," he said quietly, eyes as intense as the sudden thud of her heart, "that since that one kiss with you, Libs, I don't even want to look at another woman."

She caught her breath, the sound almost harsh in the silence as she stared at him through wide eyes, his words stunning her so much, she was barely able to breathe, much less speak.

A sheepish grin eased across his face as he idly scratched the back of his neck. "Yeah, I know, that was pretty much my reaction, too, when I finally figured it out." His gaze softened to serious as he slowly trailed his fingers down the curve of her face, the motion so achingly tender, she almost moaned. "But the truth is, no woman has ever affected me like you, Libby—*ever*—not back in school and not now, so I'm asking you to give me a chance. I know I've been a burr under your saddle till now, but I'd like to make it up to you and start all over."

A flash flood of tears welled in her eyes, slipping down her cheeks to pool in the tremble of her smile. "Oh, Finn, truly?" she whispered, hardly able to believe that the only boy she'd ever wanted, wanted her too.

"Truly." Smile gentle, he carefully traced the shape of her mouth with fingers that burned like fire, tightening her chest with a need she'd never experienced before. His smile sobered once again. "The last time I touched you, Libby, I took something that didn't belong to me, and I want you to know that I'm sorry." He wisped a gentle palm over her hair, his Adam's apple jerking hard in his throat. "But I think you should know, Miss O'Shea, that I want to kiss you right now more than I have ever wanted to kiss any woman before ..." Gaze locked with hers, he leaned in ever so slowly, halting barely a whisper away, as if intent upon giving her every chance to say no.

Problem was—she didn't *want* to say no. Because the feelings Finn McShane unleashed in her were too strong, too real, too much of what she'd longed for since she'd first met him so many years ago.

But could she trust him? Her heart stuttered in her chest.

"Libby." His breath tingled her skin, cherry-pie sweet and as ragged as hers. "I'm going to kiss you now, so if that's not what you want, then please—just push me away."

CHAPTER FOURTEEN

*P*LEASE, *LIBBY ... DON'T PUSH me away ...*
        Both his pulse and time stood still while he awaited her answer, forgetting to breathe as he watched roiling clouds of uncertainty deepen the green of her eyes. Then in a flick of her gaze to his lips and back, he sensed her consent, and tucking an arm to her waist, he slowly drew her onto his bale, closing the distance to caress her lips with his own. A lifetime of craving this girl flashed through his body like a desert heat wave, and swallowing a low groan, he molded his mouth to hers with an ache so real, he knew she was the only cure. "Libby," he whispered, pulling away to cradle her head in his hands, "I have feelings for you that go way beyond friendship or festivals, so please tell me we can start over and see where this goes."

She blinked several times, almost as if to clear the haze from her eyes, and his heart screeched to a stop. But when he saw the sweet curve of her beautiful mouth, his pulse took off in a sprint, unleashing a grin on his face he swore stretched ear to ear. "Please tell me that's a yes, Miss O'Shea, because if not, I'll have to resign as co-chair since keeping my distance will be impossible to do."

She nibbled the edge of her lips with an innocent smile, and it took everything in him not to join her, nibbling and tasting that mouth that forever invaded his thoughts. Her eyes fairly glowed as she gave him a brief nod, and there was no way he could stop the hoarse moan that scraped past his throat when he kissed her again. Sweet thunder, he was barely able to believe that he and Liberty O'Shea were on speaking terms, much less kissing like this, the heady taste of her all but melting his spurs.

Like you and Jo Beth?

Finn froze, the warmth of Libby's body against his sending an avalanche of guilt sliding right down his back, icier than the Sierras in a Nevada snowstorm. Another groan rose in his throat, but this one was because he knew he had no business taking liberties with Libby. Not when he'd been seeing mainly Jo Beth, no matter how casually or infrequent, giving into Milo's relentless prodding that Finn needed some fun in his life. True, Jo Beth wasn't the only girl he spent time with, but as Milo's girlfriend's best friend, she was the one Finn saw and liked the most.

And kissed the most?

Finn winced inwardly at the prick of his conscience. Innocent kisses with Jo Beth or any other girl had never bothered him before, but suddenly kissing Libby made them seem downright wrong. Because Libby deserved better. Shame warmed the back of his neck.

And so did Jo Beth.

He'd always prided himself on steering clear of marriage, making good and sure women knew he had no intention of courting till his land was paid off and his homestead built and settled. But looking at Libby right now—half-lidded eyes, swollen mouth, and shallow breathing from parted lips that were calling him home—he knew his days of bachelorhood were about to be cut off at the pass. With a gentle grip of her arms, he held her at bay, painfully aware that she deserved far more than a man who flirted and kissed other women, and by the grace of God, he would give it to her.

Fidelity. Marriage. And babies galore …

But first he needed to end it with Jo Beth, then give it some time to ease Jo's ruffled feathers.

And pay off your loan?

Finn's jaw tightened along with his conscience, wishing he'd broken it off with Jo Beth like he'd wanted to when rumors started to fly that he was her beau. And he would have if Milo hadn't badgered him into seeing Jo Beth more often so the four of them could be "friends" who were social together and just had a little fun.

Finn stifled a grunt. A "little fun," right. Only "friends" didn't tempt and tease with kisses like Jo Beth always did, no matter how many times he told her he had no plans to get married. But he was a man, for pity's sake, and one used to enjoying the affections of women before the Poppys had convinced him to curb his ways. And now he'd boxed himself in but good, putting so many things at risk.

Jo Beth.

Her father.

A loan that was almost paid off.

And Liberty …

A knot of conviction hitched in his throat. "Libby," he whispered, cupping her face while his thumbs glided the soft silk of her skin, "please forgive me for taking advantage of the way I feel about you, all alone up here in this loft. But I never dreamed I'd ever have a chance with you, Libs, so I guess I kind of"—he scrubbed the back of his neck with an awkward grin quickly tempered by guilt—"got carried away. But now that I know you feel the same way, I'd like to take it real slow to ward off any speculation about your reputation or mine, as co-chairs of a committee smack dab in the public eye." He battled a gulp, downright impressed with his willpower to not devour her all over again. "Do you … understand?"

She blinked several times as if she didn't while that creamy throat convulsed with a nervous bob, and he wished more than anything he could just kiss all her hesitation away. But he owed her more than kisses.

He owed her the truth.

Or at least most of it.

A tiny crimp appeared above her nose. "I'm not exactly sure what you mean by 'real slow,' Finn ..."

He skimmed a hand down that silky copper hair he'd longed to touch for too many years, fingers tingling like his heart for this girl he so wanted to make his own. "What I mean, Libby, is as co-chairs, I think we have a responsibility to be professional. And trust me, Miss O'Shea," he said with a crooked smile he hoped would help diminish the confusion in her eyes, "my feelings for you are anything but."

A silent sigh of relief leached out when a soft blush bloomed on her face, tipping that glorious mouth into the sweetest of smiles. "That said," he continued in what he hoped was a more "professional" tone, "I'd like to wait until a little while after the festival to start seeing you publicly if that's all right."

"All ... right," she said in a near whisper, the flick of her gaze to his mouth all but giving him heatstroke. "But does that mean privately too?" Her teeth nipped at those pink lips like he so longed to do while her shy smile pumped more blood through his veins.

With a gruff clear of his throat, he quickly lifted her at the waist and plopped her safely on her own bale of hay, pretty darn sure that if he didn't distance himself right now, he'd be in a whole heap of trouble. "Libby, there's something I need to tell you." He shot to his feet and started pacing, gouging the hair at the back of his head. "Before we walked into this barn, I had absolutely no hope whatsoever that my long-held dream of courting you was even a remote possibility, so when we"—his Adam's apple jerked hard as he halted to face her head-on—"kissed just now, well I ... I shouldn't have, and I'm sorry."

She rose and took a step forward, the affection in her eyes warming him to the core. "I'm not. I've felt the same way about you forever, Finn, so I'm glad the truth has finally come out."

The truth.

"Libby ..." Clearing his throat again, he retreated another step. "There's something else you need to know." He plunged his hands in his pockets, ill at ease for the first time *ever* with a girl. "As you know, I've been seeing Jo Beth here and there ..."

"Here and there?" A tiny pucker popped above her nose. "Are you ... courting her, Finn?"

Heat singed his collar when he thought of all the kisses he and Jo Beth had shared, something most women tended to construe as commitment. *Particularly* when she was the one he stepped out with the most. "No, no ... nothing like that," he was quick to respond, a niggle of concern that both Jo Beth and her father might see it differently. "I mean I like her, I do, but it's just that we've gone out a lot because of Milo, since she's Bettie's best friend and all, so some folks have assumed we're a couple." He coughed. *Especially Jo Beth and her parents.* "So what I'm saying is I'd like a chance to spare her feelings if I can." He buried his fists in his pockets once again with an awkward lift of his shoulders. "You know, give it some time for things to cool off before you and I start seeing each other that way, just to let her down easy."

She blinked, those green eyes softening to the color of new buds in early May. "I think that's very noble, Finn," she said quietly, the glow of admiration in her gaze making him feel the farthest thing from noble.

He swallowed a gulp, throat dry as dust. "Yeah, well, the thing is, Libs, I sorta promised I'd help Jo Beth celebrate her birthday on the day of the festival, if you know what I mean ..."

She blinked again, her expression indicating she didn't.

He clawed at the back of his head, sucking in more air to try and make it perfectly clear. "So I don't feel right breaking it off before then, which means it could be a while before you and I can, you know"—he wagged a finger between them—"step out together for all the town to see. So is that"—his Adam's apple did another jog—"acceptable to you?"

"More than acceptable, Finn," she said far too quickly for his ego. "Whatever you need to do is perfectly fine with me, truly, so please take your time."

Take my time? It was Finn's turn to blink. *She doesn't mind? Not even a little?* "Uh … all right, if you're sure you won't be jealous or anything—"

She was shaking her head before he could even finish the sentence. "Absolutely not," she assured him with a bright smile. "Not even a little."

"Good … good." He plunged his hands back in his pockets, not all that sure it *was* good, at least not with a girl who'd seldom shown an iota of interest till today. It was his experience that if a girl truly cared, she'd be green-eyed over any other woman. Shaking off a sliver of hurt, Finn expelled a noisy sigh. "All righty, then, Libs. Let's promise to keep this just between you and me till then. And I mean nobody else can know—not Kitty or Martha, Milo, or even Mr. and Mrs. Poppy, agreed?"

"I think that would be wise," she said with a lift of her chin. "For Jo Beth's sake."

Yeah. He tugged at his collar, desperate for more air. *And it wouldn't hurt my loan either.* Forcing a lopsided smile, he needed to make good and sure she understood he'd be treating her no differently than in the past in order to avoid any speculation about the two of them. Ignoring the uncomfortable feeling in his chest, he held out his arm, one edge of his smile jagging high. "Which means we'll revert to our prior enmity in public, Miss Bell, just to make good and sure nobody suspects a thing, agreed?"

"I suppose that would be best," she said slowly, the tiniest of puckers at the bridge of her nose, "but in private, I'd like to get to know each other better, Finn, if that's agreeable?"

He stared, pausing several seconds before slowly cupping her face in his hands, gently skimming her jaw with his thumbs. "More than agreeable," he whispered, wondering how on earth he was going to take it slow when his heart was crashing full speed ahead. He managed a crooked smile. "In fact, it might be a good idea to show up at our weekly meetings an hour earlier or so than usual. You know, just to go over things in private before everyone else arrives?"

A slow grin bloomed on her beautiful face. "I think that's an excellent idea, Mr. McShane," she said with a slow nod, green eyes sparkling as she allowed him to usher her to the ladder.

"Good." Relief breezed past his lips as he climbed down several slats, one arm extended to help her on down. "And I do believe I'm ready for something cool to drink, Libs, how 'bout you?"

"Absolutely parched, Finn, and surprisingly, a bit hungry too."

"Oh, yes, ma'am," he said, guiding her down rung by rung, her body so close, he battled hunger pains of a whole 'nother kind.

You might say—downright starved.

CHAPTER FIFTEEN

DURING THE NOON HOUR, LIBBY tapped her toe impatiently on the brand-new paver town square Zeb Miller and his boys had built, studying the empty terra cotta planters with a finger to her lips. "But sagebrush is so ... *so* ..." Notepad and pencil to her chest, she wrinkled her nose, striving to come up with a provocation that would put a burr in Finn's boot. She settled on an insult she'd once hurled at him in school when he'd called her a spoiled rich girl. Hurting people's feelings was not something she was prone to do, but Finn McShane had always managed to get under her skin, bringing out the worst in her. And before she knew it, the slur had just popped out of her mouth. *Never* had she seen Finn McShane turn that shade of red before, revealing she'd struck one of the few nerves in the cockiest boy in her class: his poor upbringing. "Pathetically common and pitifully poor," she finished with a flourish, whirling to give him her best condescending look.

His eyes narrowed considerably, and she had to bite back a smile, thinking she'd never had so much fun insulting Finn McShane before. Their "pretend" rivalry was certainly working. No one seemed even remotely aware that Finn and she had feelings for each other, not even Miss Willoughby or the ever-matchmaking Mrs. Poppy. Although Libby did feel a wee bit guilty about the older ladies' gentle reprimands and concerned glances whenever she and Finn sparred. So much so, in fact, that even Libby wondered at times if the attraction were real or if she'd only dreamed those tender kisses he'd given her since that night at the Poppys'. *Especially* since some of their heated festival disagreements since then were certainly anything *but* "pretend."

But the attraction was real, she knew, based on the countless hours they spent alone talking at City Hall *before* the meetings when they'd both arrive early. During those times, they shared about safer subjects like their hopes and dreams rather than festival business. Sometimes their talks were serious and sometimes playful, but always filled with a growing affection that was, for Libby at least, slowly ripening into love. Of course, Finn couldn't really show that when he walked her, Kitty, and Martha home after each meeting, always reverting to their usual squabbling instead. But he sure showed it when he dropped Libby off last, stealing kisses in the bushes before he delivered her to her door. Those moments together were precious to her, not only because they were some of the rare times she and Finn weren't butting heads, but because she got to see the tender and caring man behind the gruff and cocky exterior.

The *same* "gruff and cocky exterior" he now conveyed with a stubborn clamp of his mouth and an exaggerated roll of his eyes. Without question, those kisses seemed pretty distant right about now as he slacked a hip with a disgruntled fold of arms. "'Pathetically common and pitifully poor' plants that are native to our fair state, Miss O'Shea, in case you haven't noticed from the lofty height of your gilded castle."

"Now, Finn …" Mrs. Poppy said softly, obviously concerned that Libby and he intended to continue the battle of words they'd just had at City Hall.

"No, he's right, Mrs. Poppy. I have been exposed to more than pigweed and thistle since my mother adores her gardens, so we really can't blame poor Mr. McShane if he can't rise above the mundane."

A muscle twitched in Finn's sculpted face, and Libby couldn't decide if the sweat beading his brow was from the heat of the day or the heat of his temper. "I'll choose 'mundane' any day over 'dead,' *Miss Bell*, because I guarantee if you put roses in those pots, we'll end up with dead sticks."

"Not if Millie waters them twice a week," Libby insisted, grateful the mayor's secretary had volunteered to take on the task. "And the roses my mother is donating are already well established in pots, Mr. McShane, so they should transplant nicely."

"Oh absolutely," Miss Willoughby concurred with marked enthusiasm, her sentiments wholeheartedly echoed by Mrs. Poppy.

"Yeah, well I wish other things transplanted as nicely," he muttered loudly, earning a warning glare from his former teacher. He threw his hands up in the air. "Looks like I'm outnumbered—*again*. Maybe I should just go back to work where I actually have some input."

"Oh, now don't be a crab, Griffin," Mrs. Poppy said with a motherly pat of his arm, her soothing tone belied by a twinkle in her eyes. "You wouldn't have input there either if you didn't work alone, young man."

"So, it's roses in the pots and fancy wrought iron to decorate the wooden benches." Libby checked those items off her list, dismissing Finn with a bright smile. "All agreed?"

"No," Finn groused, "but does it matter?" He slapped his Stetson against his knee to clear it of dust before plopping it on his head. "Afternoon, ladies—I have *real* work to do." Without so much as a glance her way, Finn tore off down the street toward the V&T.

"Mr. McShane, wait!" Libby called after she said her goodbyes to the ladies, hurrying to catch up with Finn. "We are not done here, sir."

Finn wheeled around in the open doorway of the V&T, hand on the knob and a scowl on his face. "What is it *now*, Miss O'Shea?" he boomed, loud enough for Miss Delilah and everyone on the street and walkway to hear. "You've already taken up most of my lunch hour."

"I'd like to discuss the park benches some more." She nodded at several ladies who passed her on the boardwalk as she stopped before Finn.

"Of course you would," he said in a near growl, charging into the V&T while a wide-eyed Delilah looked on. He paused at the door of his office to glare, hands on his hips. "Let me guess—*now* you want to add little lacey pillows with hearts and flowers on them."

"Don't be ridiculous, you mule." Libby closed the front door behind her with a little too much force, sparing a strained smile in Miss Delilah's direction before she followed Finn into his office. "I want to discuss how the V&T might benefit from possibly donating a bench or two."

"For the love of mercy, Miss Bell, the V&T has already given its all to this festival, not to mention the excessive time of its director who's been hounded to death by his co-chair." He turned his back on her to storm to his desk, grumbling all the way.

"You want hounded?" Libby slammed his office door behind her with a rattle of the glass and marched right around his desk. "I'll show you 'hounded.'"

"Oh yes, ma'am, *please*—'hound' away," Finn said in her ear as he butted her to the wall with a low groan, smothering her neck with kisses. "Heaven help me, I've missed you, Libby."

Near melting, Libby matched his groan with a weak one of her own before she raised her voice several octaves, hopefully loud enough for Miss Delilah to hear through the closed door. "You're going to miss more than that, Mr. McShame, if you don't sit down right now and listen to me, so *SIT!*"

"With pleasure." Finn grinned as he eased back on his desk, tugging Libby along while he pressed a kiss to her hair, arms securely around her waist. "So, speak to me, Miss O'Shea," he whispered, thumb grazing the small of her back.

"Welllllll ..." Excitement bubbling inside, Libby toyed with the edge of Finn's string tie with a shy smile. "I thought of a great way to pay for the four benches, Finn, but I wanted to check with you first before I proposed it to the rest of the committee."

He crooked a dark brow, mouth veering off-center as he tugged on a lock of her hair. "What? Make V&T pay for them all?"

"Not *all* of them, silly," she said with a soft giggle, "but whoever does donate a bench will have the honor of claiming it as their own with a brass plate right on top for all to see." She tipped her head with a nervous chew of her lip. "So ... what do you think?"

He drew her close to graze her lips with a slow and lingering kiss. "I think you're flat-out adorable, Co-chair O'Shea, and I'm all for 'claiming' something as my own." He burrowed his lips into the crook of her neck, skimming kisses all the way up to the soft flesh of her ear. "And I'm sure not talking benches," he breathed, his words warm against her throat while he tenderly suckled her lobe.

"Focus, McShane!" she shouted in a near gasp, her breathing ragged as she prodded him back with a hazy smile. "So my idea—do you like it? The engraver at the newspaper said he could make the brass plates if you do."

"I love it," he said, depositing a kiss to the tip of her nose. "And the bench idea is nice too." Giving her a tight squeeze, he stood to his feet and slowly ushered her to the door. "You need to scoot before somebody gets suspicious, but put the V&T down for one bench, Libs, and I'll make Milo pick up another for the newspaper."

"Excellent, Director Finn!" She reached for the door

knob, smile radiant. "I can't thank you enough."

"Sure you can," he said softly, the heat in his eyes unleashing more than a little heat of her own. He gently nudged her against the wall with a half-lidded look that made her throat go dry, turning her bones to butter when he slowly tugged and toyed her mouth with his before delving in deeper. His voice was a husky rasp when he finally pulled away. "And someday soon, I hope."

Breathless from the warmth purling through her body, she glanced up, voice far too frail. "How soon?"

His manner sobered considerably as he quietly slipped several curls over her shoulder, his gaze focused on his fingers rather than on her face. "I honestly don't know right now, Libby, but I'm working on it, I promise." He finally looked up, eyes tender. "I just think we need to give it a decent amount of time beyond the festival, so can you trust me a little while longer?"

Libby swallowed the disappointment clogging her throat. "Sure, Finn."

"Thank you." He bent to graze her forehead with a tender kiss. "Then I'll see you early at our final meeting before setup, all right?" He moved to open the door, hand on the knob as he gave her a wink before his smile slashed into a scowl. "Fine—have it your way, Miss O'Shea," he bellowed as he opened it wide, "you usually do."

"Oh, you're just impossible," she shouted back, head high as she marched out of his office. "This festival can't come soon enough to suit me, I can tell you that."

"I couldn't agree more," a feminine voice said sharply from behind, and Libby spun around to see Jo Beth in front of Miss Delilah's desk. She pinned Libby with a superior glare as she swished past with her nose in the air. "Everyone knows how you've badgered poor Finn throughout this entire process, so I guarantee, Liberty O'Shea, you won't be the only one relieved when it's done." Her voice suddenly melted into warm honey as she placed a possessive hand on Finn's arm. "Finn, Mama made all of your favorite dishes for my birthday dinner before the dance, so be sure to come hungry."

Finn's gaze flicked to Libby and back, his firm tone clearly at odds with the ruddy rash bleeding up the back of his neck.

"Sorry, Jo Beth, but I have festival responsibilities to attend to before the dance."

"But it's my birthday," she said with a pout in her voice, "and you promised to help make it the best celebration ever, remember? Besides," she said with a haughty glance over her shoulder, "Liberty won't mind because everyone knows she likes to run the show."

Finn gave a gruff clear of his throat. "I wish I could, Jo Beth, but I'm co-chair—"

"Humpf. If *that's* what you want to call it." Libby's voice rose in volume, all prior patience and understanding regarding Jo Beth suddenly going up in smoke along with her temper. "Frankly, I'm used to you shirking your responsibilities, Mr. McShane," she snapped, enough sparks burning in her eyes to rival the fireworks display planned in the new town square. "So what's one more?"

"See?" Smile smug, Jo Beth hooked her arm through Finn's, the look of adoration on her face enough to make Libby lose her lunch. "Now we can celebrate my birthday as planned."

As planned.

"Jo Beth, I'm really sorry, but I can't—"

"Oh, sure you can!" Libby marched to the door, grappling for the knob while her fury rose faster than the blood in her cheeks. Smile stiff, she turned, her notorious rivalry with Finn coming in awfully handy as she jutted her chin to scorch him with a glare. "You're more hindrance than help half the time anyway, so be my guest, please. After all, you *did* promise Jo Beth, Mr. McShane," she said, horrified at the unexpected moisture that stung at the back of her lids, "and we all know you don't break promises." She slammed the door hard, hand shaking as she swiped at her eyes.

Just hearts.

CHAPTER SIXTEEN

"YOU KNOW, LIBS, YOU'RE AWFULLY crabby for someone who just organized the most successful fundraiser Nevada has ever had." Serving lemonade at the checkered-clad refreshment table at the back of the barn, Kitty nodded toward a split-log plank dance floor crowded with people. Intimately lit by a host of glowing lanterns strung high in the rafters like stars in the sky, ladies in frilly bonnets and finery danced with cowboys in their Sunday best. *Minus* spurs, guns, and hats, of course—one of the few battles Libby had actually won with Finn McShane.

Expelling a noisy sigh, Libby was well aware that her best friend was right—she was crabby. She breathed in the magic of the Poppys' cozy barn. The earthy scent of hay, cider, and newly hewn cedar tables and benches warmed her as much as the array of lanterns illuminating a sea of smiling faces. Her body fairly buzzed with the lively sounds of banjos and fiddles—Finn's choice, of course—but she'd won on the violin and cello, all harmonizing beautifully with the laughter of adults and the giggles of children. She absently tapped her toe to the music provided by a host of bearded musicians on the log-slatted stage, almost wishing she had said yes to the various men who'd asked her to dance. But she had too much to do, so she opted to enjoy it all from afar.

She slid a secret look Finn's way while he laughed with Jo Beth.

But apparently not far enough.

Rib cage expanding, she tried to dispel the niggle of a headache with another deep inhale. The strain in her temples eased somewhat as she took in the sweet smell of sawdust and pipe tobacco. She sighed. Unfortunately it occasionally mingled with the faint hint of horses and too many men in a crowded barn. She wrinkled her nose, hating to admit Finn had been right. The pretty wall of quilts she'd pinned on a clothesline to cordon off supplies at the rear door had obviously restricted airflow. Her gaze narrowed as Finn whispered in Jo Beth's ear.

By thunder, I'd like to restrict a little airflow right about now …

Lips compressed, she turned her attention away from Finn, expelling a weary sigh. Oh well, in spite of the somewhat overly ripe masculine smell, no question that today—the first day of the festival, July 3rd—had gone off like clockwork. From the baking contest, picnic auction, and full day of fun and games at the booths, to this evening's bake sale and barn dance at the Poppys', each appeared to be a rousing success. And never had the town seen a more dazzling array of booths! A satisfied smile inched its way across Libby's lips as she thought of their schoolhouse education booth. It was wildly popular, from bobbing for apples and mini spelling bees, to games of tic-tac-toe and gallows on the makeshift blackboard. *Not* to mention the best candy apples Libby ever made.

Her annoyance at Finn over Jo Beth resurfaced when she remembered how everyone had raved about Finn's booth as well. The show-off actually managed to tow a real steam engine to the field with Milo's help and a team of horses, on loan from the V&T. Not only had the judges gushed over Finn's resourcefulness, but everyone fawned over the "brilliance" of giving tours through a real engine car. Mothers were thrilled their children could learn how a steam engine actually worked while children were awe-struck over the chance to tug on the whistle and billow steam into the air. Finn had become an instant hero as usual, awarding horsey rides to the children waiting in line and perilous smiles to their mothers. Libby's headache kicked up a notch.

Rubbing a pain in her temple, she once again forced her attention away from the frustration of Finn to the truly outstanding festival the town had put on. From dignitaries and out-of-town visitors, to townsfolk anxious to show off their hometown pride, everything was in place for a Fourth of July festival like no other. All capped off tomorrow, of course, with a horse race, booth contest, potluck, talent show, parade, and the best fireworks display in the West.

So why am I so crabby?

She stifled a grunt as she chanced another peek at Finn while he danced with Jo Beth for the third blasted time, and had no doubt whatsoever as to the cause for the burr in her saddle. Her co-chair was doling out dances to the ladies of Virginia City faster than she and Kitty could dole out lemonade, leaving a sour taste in Libby's mouth that was anything but sweet.

More like cold and tart.

Jo Beth's scarlet dress spun wide as Finn whirled her to the lively sound of "Yankee Doodle," and Libby's mouth went flat. He'd said he wanted to wait till after the festival to spare Jo Beth's feelings, but it sure looked to Libby like he was sparing a whole lot more than that. The very thought sent the heat in her cheeks straight to her temper as she snatched up a cup of lemonade served in punch glasses on loan from ladies in the town. Tilting it straight up, she guzzled like it was the cornpone whiskey she'd banned from the festival grounds.

Because despite his ardent confession at the Poppys' a month ago that he didn't "even want to look at another woman," *and* his secret attention and kisses ever since, Finn *McPain* was not only *still* seeing Jo Beth, he appeared to be enjoying it as well. When he'd told her he wanted to "take it slow" to spare Jo Beth's feelings, she had thought him noble. Now after four weeks of pining for a former archenemy she hadn't even liked in the beginning, it bordered more on …

Ignoble.

She stifled a grunt. And now here he was, dancing with everybody but her—from Mrs. Poppy and Miss Willoughby, to every other lovesick female in the room, age three to eighty-three. Yes, she was proud of the job they'd done with the festival, certainly, but the bald-faced truth was that from the moment Finn *McShame* had kissed her and declared his intentions, the man had put a hornet in her hat that she sorely wished she could sic right back on him. Because just *seeing* Jo Beth in the V&T office earlier in the week had unleashed a sting of jealousy so strong, it felt like a whole hive of hornets a buzzin' in her brain. And to make matters worse, their private time before the final meeting had been invaded by anxious volunteers arriving early for setup, including a fawning Jo Beth.

Leaving Finn and Libby no time alone since.

Catching her glaring, Finn actually had the nerve to toss her a wink, and Libby's face flashed so hot, she snatched another lemonade and spun around, tempted to cool off with a douse instead of a drink. Draining the glass, she turned to slam it back down on the makeshift table, wobbling all the others Kitty and Martha had just filled.

"See? Crabby," her best friend said again, tugging her away from the drink table. "You have turned down every man that has asked you to dance tonight, Libs, opting to hide out back here instead." Bracing Libby's arms, Kitty seared her with a probing look. "I've seen this kind of mood in you before, Liberty O'Shea, and somehow it always has to do with Finn, so confess." Tone softening, Kitty wiggled her brows. "Did that boy try to kiss you again?"

Libby was sure Jo Beth's dress had nothing on her when

warmth whooshed into her face, red-hot.

"I knew it!" Kitty dipped her knees with a squeal and swallowed Libby up in a hug, pulling back with a mischievous grin. "That bad boy did, didn't he?"

Mortified, Libby snuck a peek over her shoulder to where "that bad boy" was casually strolling toward their table in his best vest and string tie. Hands in his pockets, he flashed that annoying crooked grin that always tumbled Libby's stomach.

"Evenin', Kitty, Martha ..." He paused to deliver a slow smile in Libby's direction, eyes twinkling as his gaze lowered to her mouth with a husky drawl. "Libby."

A hot retort teetered on the tip of her tongue, near as scalding as the fire in her cheeks.

"Why, there you are, Finn McShane," Jo Beth's mother interrupted, sidling over to loop an arm through Finn's while her entourage of ladies' guild members—all judges for the booth contest—gathered around. "I do declare— if your booth wasn't the most creative and clever in the festival, I'll eat my hat." Mrs. Templeton delivered a butterscotch grin with a bat of her eyes.

Libby turned away to retrieve a fresh jug of lemonade, wishing Jo Beth's mother *would* eat her feather hat.

And maybe choke a wee bit ...

"Why, thank you, Mrs. Templeton," Finn said with that infuriating smile in a husky voice that could charm fleas off a dog. "I'm happy to say we had a pretty fair turnout, yielding a healthy donation for our town." Glancing over his shoulder, he flashed a grin at Liberty, Kitty, and Martha. "Although I believe these girls here gave us a run for our money."

Nose wrinkling, Mrs. Templeton averted her head slightly to offer a smile to Libby that was more of a smirk. "Yes, but I'm afraid my Harold choking on that apple from the dunking booth could possibly cost them some points in the contest."

Libby's eyes narrowed considerably. Suddenly she smelled a rotten apple.

"Oh and Finn," Mrs. Templeton said with another flutter of lashes that reminded Libby a little too much of her daughter, "Jo Beth wondered if you might bring her a lemonade. I do believe you wore my girl plum out with so many dances, so she's quite parched."

I'll show her parched. Libby swiped the jug, sloshing lemonade into empty glasses.

"My pleasure, Mrs. Templeton." Finn promptly picked up two punch cups, handing Martha his payment before turning to go.

But not before sliding Libby another wink.

"Did you see that?" Kitty whispered loudly when Mrs. Templeton and crew had taken their leave. "Finn winked at you, Libs— again!" She tapped her toe with a firm fold of arms, a smile squirming on her lips. "I don't think you're telling me everything that's going on here, because I sure don't see that man winking at anybody else. Which is downright peculiar since everybody thinks he and Jo Beth are a horse hair away from courting."

A horse hair away from courting.

Libby's brows dug low. *More like a horse's behind* ... "First of all, Kit," she said in a clipped voice, "Finn McShane is a shameless scoundrel who will flirt with anything in a skirt, so a wink from a man like that means absolutely nothing." Her eyes thinned as she glowered in his direction. *Except heartbreak.* "And secondly, not only is he *not* courting Jo Beth, but he has no plans to do so."

"And just how would you know that?" Kitty asked with a purse of a smile. "*Unless* he *told you* when he kissed you?"

"He didn't tell me anything," she fibbed, ignoring Kitty's reference to a kiss while she seared Finn and Jo Beth with a steel-eyed squint. *Except, obviously, a pack of lies.* She huffed out a noisy sigh. "Look, Kitty, you told me yourself he's been seeing Jo Beth more than anyone else for a long time now, so I just figured if he hasn't made a move yet, I doubt he will."

Kitty bumped a shoulder against Libby's, a gleam of trouble in her eyes. "So, has he?"

Libby tore her gaze from Finn to blink at her best friend. "Has he what?"

"Made a move!" Kitty emphasized loudly under her breath.

A grunt rolled from Libby's lips as she checked the watch pinned to her bodice. She snatched the cashbox from under the table, determined to avoid her best friend's inquisition by collecting the money from the dessert table. "Apparently that's a question for Jo Beth," she bit out.

"Ah-hah!" Kitty blocked her way with a cheeky grin. "*Apparently?* Mmm ... that sounds a little bit like sour lemonade to me, doesn't it, Martha?"

Martha nodded shyly, teeth tugging her lip.

Kitty cocked her head to deliver a sly look. "You know—like maybe you're a wee bit ... jealous?"

"Of Jo Beth *Templeton?*" Libby gaped, eyes as round as the silver dollars in her cashbox. A lump suddenly bobbed in her throat when she realized that Kitty was probably right. Her eyelids shuttered closed at the absurd idea that she would *ever* be jealous over Finn McShane. But apparently the man had—*once again*—bamboozled her. Like all the pranks he'd played on her in school, he'd obviously done it again—won her trust so he could set her up for the fall. A weak groan scraped past her lips as she put a quivering hand to her eyes.

The fall.

And heaven help her, this time she'd fallen hard.

"Libs?" Kitty gently brushed hair from Libby's face, her tone soft with understanding. "You're in love with him, aren't you?"

Tears sprang to Libby's eyes as she stared at her best friend. "I never meant for it to happen, Kit," she whispered, "but he's been so nice to me ever since the night we had dinner at the Poppys' when he told me he didn't even want to look at another woman."

"*What?*" The whites of Kitty's and Martha's eyes all but bulged in shock.

"And then, of course, there's all those kisses he's given me since ..."

Her friends squealed in unison. "I knew it!" Kitty crowed, giving Libby a tight hug. "You've been walking on air since you went to the Poppys' that night, so I just *knew* something happened." Her brows dipped low. "Even *though* our best friend refused to divulge a single thing anytime we asked."

"I'm sorry, Kit, Martha, but Finn swore me to secrecy because he said he wanted to let Jo Beth down easy after he broke it off." Her eyes narrowed to slits as she watched Jo Beth sitting so close to Finn, the woman may as well sit on his blasted lap. "Which is exactly what I'd like to do right about now—let *him* 'down easy.'" She grunted. "In a well filled with devil-tree thorns and cactus."

"Ouch." Kitty glanced Finn's way, her gaze suddenly as flat as her smile. "I reckon he deserves it, though, with the way he's been fawning over Jo Beth all night."

"Well, not *all* night, Kitty," Martha said in a timid voice, sympathy etched in her face. "Finn's danced with pert near every woman here tonight, Libs, 'cept you, Kitty, and me."

"Uh-oh." Kitty nudged Libby's arm. "Looks like he may be a fixin' to correct that."

Libby whirled around, knees all but giving way when she saw Finn striding toward them with two empty punch cups, looking more handsome than a womanizing coyote had a right. He set the cups down and doffed his Stetson. "Ladies—now that this shindig is almost over, I just realized I forgot to dance with the three prettiest girls here tonight."

Libby fought the inclination to roll her eyes while Martha

blushed. Even Kitty, for once, appeared to be tongue-tied. Finn's gaze roved from each of their faces and back with that slow, easy smile that always made Libby's stomach a little too dizzy. Her lips tamped in a hard smile. *Good.* Maybe she could puke all over his rawhide boots.

"So, who's willing to dance with a rakish but lovable cowboy?" Finn said in a husky drawl that was annoyingly reinforced by a flash of dimples.

Not me. Libby crossed her arms with resolve, grateful that at least she and her two sensible friends would turn this blackguard away, even if every other woman swooned at his feet.

"I will!" Apparently Kitty had found her tongue because she bolted around the refreshment station like Finn had just proposed, shimmying the lemonade in all the cups.

Libby's jaw dropped as she watched her best friend scurry to Finn's side, hooking her arm to his before shooting Libby a sheepish smile. "Sorry, Libs, but I haven't danced once tonight since working the refreshment table, so I hope you don't mind …?"

"Naw, she doesn't mind, do you, Libs?" He had the audacity to wink, those hazel eyes twinkling with tease. "Because once I dance with Kitty and Martha, you might just get your turn, too, Miss Bell. After all, patience is a mighty attractive virtue, ma'am, so you can just thank me later."

CHAPTER SEVENTEEN

FINN HAD AN AWFULLY TOUGH time keeping his grin in check while he danced with Martha, the look on Liberty's face enough to puff his chest out with pride. Pinched lips, clamped jaw, and gushing lemonade in cups like it was a drought in the Mohave.

Even though Libby was the celebrated mastermind behind Virginia City's most successful and far-reaching fundraiser, his pretty co-chair appeared downright peeved. His grin broke through despite his best efforts. And he had a sneaking suspicion why.

The woman is flat-out crazy about me.

Smiling, he gave Martha an extra whirl at the end of their dance because deep down he was as giddy as a schoolboy that Liberty Margaret O'Shea apparently cared about him as much as he cared about her, sweet vindication after years of secret pining.

Of course, he hadn't *meant* to make her mad when he'd danced with Jo Beth more than anyone else, but it was Jo's birthday after all, and he'd long ago promised both Jo *and* Milo that he'd make sure it was a good one. Besides, Liberty had made it more than clear it didn't bother her a whit.

"Whatever you need to do is perfectly fine with me, truly, so please take your time."

A slow smile slid across his lips. Because she *said* she wasn't jealous. *"Not even a little."*

He grinned outright. *Nope, more like a lot.* And tonight when he'd danced with every girl in the place except her, on top of Jo Beth three times, he could feel that green-eyed glare singe the hairs on the back of his neck.

His mood tempered somewhat at the thought of causing Liberty distress, but this was their agreement, after all, and the only way to throw everyone off the track. Holy thunder, Mrs. Poppy just cornered him this morning, asking if he'd thought anymore about pursuing Liberty. Finn stifled a grunt. Was the woman serious? Day and night he "thought" about pursuing Liberty and then some, but he wanted to do it guilt-free, putting enough distance and time between him and Jo Beth to cushion Jo's feelings *and* pay off the debt he owed to her father. And he was almost there. Between the prize money for the booth and the bonus Superintendent Yerington promised if V&T won, he and Liberty would be able to start out with a clean slate.

No guilt.

No debt.

No butting heads with the woman he loved.

Unlike now. He flashed some teeth Liberty's way as he escorted Martha back to the table, wishing he didn't have to play this game. But then on the other hand—he grinned—who knew jealousy could feel so dad-burned good?

"Thank you, ladies, for the dances," he said as he returned Martha to the refreshment table, chuckling outright when Liberty turned her back on them to drown several dirty cups in a wash bucket.

"It was fun, Finn, so thank *you*," Kitty responded while Martha managed a shy nod, "but it looks like there's still one girl you haven't danced with yet." She nudged Liberty's shoulder, and Finn chuckled when Liberty elbowed her in return with a little too much force.

"Last square dance of the night, folks," the lead fiddler called, "so grab your partner for 'Turkey in the Straw.'"

"So what do you say, Miss Bell—ready to take a whirl?" And, oh, she "whirled" all right—like a prairie twister ready to tear him apart, limb by limb. Slapping her hands to her hips, she cauterized him with a glare thinner than a blade of prairie grass and just as sharp. "I wouldn't dance with you if you threatened me at gunpoint, Finn Mc*Vain*, so why don't you go ply your charms elsewhere?" With a spin of her heel, she refocused on washing cups, accidentally bumping Kitty in the process. "Sorry, Kit," she muttered.

A grin tickled Finn's lips. Either the woman was one fine actress, playing along with a stage-worthy imitation of their prior feud, or flat-out jealous, neither of which bode well for his boots if he actually got her out on the floor. "Well, I left my gun at the door as requested, Miss O'Shea, so I can't threaten you, but Mrs. Poppy *did* suggest that the co-chairs partnering for the final square dance would be most fitting."

"You want fitting?" She swung back around, dishwater flying everywhere when the cup in her hand flung with the motion. "I think nailing your boots to the floor with you in them would be 'fitting,' Mr. *McPain*, but I'm not going to do *that* either."

He took a quick step back, wiggling his toes for good measure. "Aw, come on, Libs," he said in a softer tone, employing his fail-proof, little-boy smile, "let's give the people a show."

"A show?" Those green eyes spanned wide as she splayed a hand to her bodice. "Why certainly, Mr. McShane, I'll be happy to give them a show! Just let me clean up a bit." Putting the cup down, she turned away to repin a few stray curls from an alabaster neck he *so* craved to taste, then smoothed a palm down the skirt of her dress like he *so* longed to do.

Ker-splash!!

Finn blinked, completely caught off-guard by dirty water

sluicing down his face onto his favorite shirt. Liberty stood there with an empty bucket in her hand and a smirk on her face while the raucous sounds of "Turkey in the Straw" boomed to the rafters.

"Turkey in the straw, turkey in the hay, turkey in the straw, what do you say?"

Giggles rose from Kitty and Martha as he swiped a sleeve across his wet face, about as speechless as that blasted turkey in the dad-burned blasted hay.

Liberty stared him down with heat in her eyes. "Because if you think I'm going to dance with you, mister, you are all wet, so go drip somewhere else." Slamming her empty bucket down, she snagged a towel and balled it up, pelting it at his chest before glancing at her friends. "Martha, Kitty—if you'd be kind enough to scatter hay on the wet mud, I'd be much obliged. Obviously I need more water." She seized the bucket and sparing him one last nasty look, stormed through the wall of quilts and out the back door.

"Good heavens, Finn," Kitty said with an innocent flutter of lashes, "what on earth did you do to light a fire under our Libby like that?"

"Can't say, ladies, but I can tell you this ..." Smile tight, Finn plucked the towel from the floor and swabbed his shirt and vest, grateful the crowd was focused on the rousing dance instead of on him. Tossing the towel on the table, he slapped his Stetson on and strode toward the back door. "I sure in the devil plan to do it again."

CHAPTER EIGHTEEN

WOMAN, YOU ARE A HANDFUL. The back barn door squealed closed behind Finn as he squinted in the dark. *But I am more than up to the challenge.* Barely waiting for his eyes to adjust, he barreled toward Mrs. Poppy's pump at the back of the house, pretty sure Liberty would go there rather than the well out in front. He smiled at a passel of kids sailing on rope swings, then nodded at older townsfolk rockin' on the front porch. Lanterns lit up the lawn for games of checkers around wood stumps while lines of people waited at the far treeline beside outhouses built especially for the festival.

Rounding the corner of the back porch, he paused, Mrs. Poppy's pump deserted in the moonlight, silent and still. Head cocked, he scanned both garden and yard, straining to hear over the trill of tree frogs and the faraway sound of the hoedown.

"Blue blazes, Libby, where the devil are you?" he mumbled to himself, well aware he didn't have much time before he needed to get back. Closing his eyes, he halted, focusing hard on sounds in the backyard.

And then he heard it. The faintest hitch of someone crying, coming straight from the Poppys' personal outhouse at the far corner of the yard. A faint sniffle harpooned straight through his heart, and guilt immediately doused any frustration she'd riled with the stupid bucket of water. With as much stealth as he could muster, he made his way to the shed and quietly tapped on the door. "Libby, I know you're in there, so will you open up please?"

"Go away, I don't want to dance." The nasal pout in her voice made him smile.

Head bowed, Finn butted a shoulder to the door. "Good, because neither do I. I want to talk."

"Well, I don't want to talk either, Finn McShane, so just *go away.*"

"Can't," he said with a heavy sigh that sealed his fate. "Because those tears you're crying are tearing me up."

She sniffed. "Why? Because you're guilty as sin?"

He expelled a noisy breath, wishing with everything in him he could just court her the way that he wanted. "No, darlin', because I'm pretty darn sure I'm in love with you."

"Horse apples!" she shouted, and he grinned when she kicked the door.

He rattled the latch, which she'd secured on the inside. "Come on, Libs, open up so we can talk face-to-face, please?"

"No. Go talk to Jo Beth, you low-down, womanizing skunk."

Finn banged his head against the door. "You are making me crazy, you know that?"

"Good!" she yelled through the crack. "You've made me crazy for years, so why don't you go back to your crowd of admirers?"

Finn slammed a palm to the door, his voice a harsh whisper. "Because I don't give a rat's tail who admires me, Liberty O'Shea. The only reason I paid any mind to any girl tonight is to throw people off that I care about *you,* so you may as well open up because I sure don't want to break the door."

"Ha! The only thing you're good at breaking are women's hearts, you … you … letch!"

"Okay, that's it." Finn scoured the ground for a stick. Muttering under his breath, he snapped one off a tree and rammed it beneath the latch of the outhouse that *he* built for the Poppys, flipping the wooden bar with ease. He yanked the door open, and Liberty jumped back, almost falling onto the wooden commode. Latching onto her wrist, he dragged her outside and around the back, ignoring her hissing and harping as he pinned her to a tree. "So help me, Libby, you are going to hear me out if I have to die trying," he said, tone rough.

"Good! That's the best idea you've had yet!" She broke free, nails flailing. "I'll bet Jo Beth will cry a bucket of tears, and if she's smart, she'll throw them right on your casket."

"Whoa!" Finn quickly immobilized her, risking life and limb to cut loose with a grin. He gentled his hold. "You know, Liberty Bell, if I didn't know better, I'd think you were jealous."

"*I'll-give-you-jealous—*" Battling tooth and nail, she jerked her knee up with a grunt.

He dodged her thrust and braced her to the tree once again, his laughter husky and low as he gave her a crooked smile. "Come on, Libs, admit it—you've fallen for me, haven't you?" She growled and tried to knee him again, and he locked her with his leg. "Because I sure have fallen for you, darlin'." He lowered to tease her earlobe with a playful tug of his teeth, then laughed out loud when she bucked like a bronc in a red-hot stall. "I want to court you, Libby," he said with a chuckle before he silenced her with a kiss so deep, there was no room for protest. Her thrashing slowed as she went limp against the tree, chest heaving as hard as his when he finally gave her some air.

His breathing was as shallow as hers when he forced his gaze from those wet, parted lips up to moss-colored eyes, hazy with desire even in the moonlight. "I know it didn't look like it tonight, Libby, but I'm crazy about you, sweetheart, and I know from that kiss that you're crazy about me too. So all I'm asking is you give me a little time to settle my affairs, and then I'll marry you so fast, your head will spin."

"It already is," she muttered, voice breathless and lips in a pout.

Gaze soft, he cradled her face in his hands. "Oh, honey, you haven't seen anything yet," he whispered, bending in to slowly nuzzle her neck, "but you have my solemn word, Miss O'Shea—you will." Eyes sheathing closed, he lowered to seal it with a kiss.

Two palms rammed hard against his chest, pushing him away. "What about Jo Beth?" she rasped, eyes as glazed as his.

He gulped, the dilemma he faced dousing some of the heat in his blood. Today was Jo Beth's birthday, so he didn't have the heart to end it with her tonight, especially when he'd promised to take her home for cake with her family. Instead, he'd planned to tell her a week or so after the festival, giving her time to calm down and him a chance to pay off the loan.

But looking at Liberty now, he knew he needed to do it sooner rather than later for both women's sakes. *And* for his own self-respect, he realized, even though it might jeopardize that stupid loan. Sucking in a deep breath, he gently fondled a silky strand of her hair, his gaze soft with regret. "I'm working on it, Libs, I promise, so I'm asking you to trust me."

She arched a brow. "Trust you." Those beautiful lips quirked in an off-center smile. "The boy who put a worm in my coat pocket and snails in my lunch pail?"

He managed a sheepish smile. "That was the old Griffin McShane. The new one is out-right crazy about you, Miss O'Shea, and hog-tied in love." He pressed a kiss to her nose. "Gotta go, Libs, but I guarantee it'll be worth the wait." He brushed a tender kiss to her lips before turning to leave.

"It better be, McShane," she called after him, "or you're in a whole heap of trouble."

Mouth dry, Finn strode back to the barn with a lump in his throat as "sticky" as the situation he'd somehow backed himself into. He sure didn't need Liberty O'Shea to remind him he'd be in trouble, because deep down he had a gut-gnawing suspicion ...

He already was.

CHAPTER NINETEEN

"I THINK TONIGHT'S THE NIGHT."

Liberty froze behind the wall of quilts as she counted the evening's food and drink proceeds, Jo Beth's whisper capturing her attention.

Bettie Boswell squealed. "How do you know?"

"Because it's my birthday, silly, and because Nellie Sue told Kristi Lemp that Finn came in to the mercantile a few weeks ago and"—Jo Beth giggled and did a little hop— "bought a wedding ring for me! So I think that gorgeous man is finally going to propose."

Liberty went stone still while the shadows beneath the quilt danced for joy.

A throaty laugh drifted beneath the comforter wall. "Besides," Jo Beth whispered in a sultry tone, "a man doesn't kiss a woman like Finn McShane kissed me the last time we all went to dinner unless he's serious, remember?"

"How could I forget?" Bettie said with a sly chuckle. "You had razor burn for a solid week."

Razor burn. Liberty's eyelids shuddered closed, experiencing a little "razor burn" herself, slicing right through her heart.

Jo Beth released a heavy sigh. "I know, and don't forget Milo told you Finn wouldn't even think about marriage until his land was free and clear and the silver mine up and running. Well, his loan is almost paid off—"

"Thanks to *you*," Bettie interjected, "sealing the deal

with the best rate in town."

Sealing the deal. Liberty slowly sank onto a hay bale while tears welled in her eyes, the memory of her father's words piercing her to the core.

"He's nothing but a womanizer and fortune hunter, I tell you, selling his soul to George Templeton, no doubt sealing the deal by courting his daughter."

"I know, although that man is so darn stubborn, can you believe he actually balked at first?" Jo Beth asked, disbelief threading her tone. "Thank goodness Daddy explained it was his way of investing in Finn's mine." She huffed out a sigh. "Apparently legitimate investment is the only way to get around Finn McShane's pride. *Which* is why Daddy has promised further investment down the road, claiming Finn is 'more of a son than a client.'"

Bettie squealed again, her shadow hugging Jo Beth's. "Oh, Jo, Finn would be a fool not to propose!" she gushed. "And I am so excited Milo and I will be there tonight to see it!"

"I know!" Jo Beth's voice turned sour. "And we could have been on our way right after the dance if that snotty Liberty O'Shea hadn't insisted Finn and Milo stay and clean up. I never could stand her, always actin' like she's so all-fire smart, and she's even worse now with that fancy degree." Her annoyance blasted out in a noisy sigh. "I don't know how Finn can stand working with the woman, as downright bossy as she is."

Bettie leaned close to Jo Beth, her voice lowering to the level of gossip. "Milo says she drives poor Finn crazy, butting heads over every little thing, but Finn knows how to handle her."

Jo Beth snickered. "How? With a bit and bridle?"

"Nope, he just rails right back when she gives him trouble, apparently, which according to Milo is as often as the sun sets and rises. Claims Finn said she's a spinster in the making."

Nausea curdled Liberty's stomach.

"You girls ready to go?"

The blood instantly drained from Liberty's face at the sound of Finn's voice, her body flushing hot and then cold. Milo's chuckle carried over the quilt. "Imagine they are, Finn, since there's a triple layer chocolate cake just waitin' for us over at Jo Beth's."

Finn's husky laughter shrank Liberty's ribcage till she thought she couldn't breathe. "That's right. We have an awful lot to celebrate tonight, Miss Templeton, so let's see if we can't make this the best birthday ever."

"Oh, I hope so," Jo Beth said with a soft giggle, all voices fading as the two couples obviously made their way to the front of the barn.

Body numb, Liberty slumped on the hay bale, head in her hands while tears stung in her eyes. Bettie had said Finn would be a fool not to propose and she was right. Finn McShane was a lot of things—a rogue, a tease, and a tyrant among them—but the man was definitely no fool. Her heart broke in two as a sob wrenched from her lips.

No, that title belonged to her.

CHAPTER TWENTY

"OH MY GOODNESS—I CAN HARDLY believe we won!" Kitty said with a giggle while she, Martha, and Liberty admired the 1st-Place ribbon that fluttered at the front of their schoolhouse booth.

"I know." Liberty's tone was lackluster. She should have been giddy with excitement like the swarms of children buzzing the festival grounds after too much rock candy, but somehow the win was bittersweet.

Somehow? Libby cast a razor-thin peek over her shoulder at Finn's booth, where a host of children and ladies still hovered despite the fact that all booths were now closed for the potluck.

Martha gently brushed the blue ribbon, a look of awe shining on her face. "I honestly didn't think we'd stand a chance since Finn's booth is so amazing, but I'm overjoyed we did." She looped her arm through Libby's. "What are you going to do with your share of the award money, Libby?"

Hire a gunslinger. "I'd like to donate it to the National American Woman Suffrage Association, I think." *So women can put reprobates like Finn McShane in their place.*

"I'm going to buy that dress I've been drooling over in Mort's Mercantile," Kitty said with a thrust of her chin, "then donate the rest to Pastor and Mrs. Poppy for that church bell they've been wanting so badly." She looped an arm around Martha's waist. "How 'bout you, Martha?"

Martha sighed. "I would love to buy a year's supply of Mrs. Poppy's award-winning cake because nobody bakes like the pastor's wife."

Kitty laughed. "I'm with you there. Mrs. Poppy's cakes always give me a warm, satisfied feeling inside, so it's no wonder she wins hands-down every single year." She nudged Liberty's shoulder with her own. "Sorry your chocolate fudge pie came in second, Libs, but at least you get to enjoy Mrs. Poppy's award-winning cake at her house later tonight. *And* with the most handsome man in town to boot."

"Not if I can help it," Libby muttered, eyes narrowing when another glimpse at the V&T booth revealed the blackguard was flirting his fool head off.

Kitty blinked, confusion furrowing her brow. "But I thought you said you and Finn talked everything out last night. That you were looking forward to seeing him at the Poppys' after the fireworks so you could serve him a piece of your famous chocolate fudge pie."

"We did," Liberty said with a tight smile. "And I most definitely am." Her gaze was a knife point. *Laced with a double dose of ipecac.*

"All this talk about food is making me hungry," Martha said, "so we should probably close up and go to the pot-luck."

Liberty checked the watch pinned to her bodice. "Great balls of fire! I need to round up those performing in the talent show to give them final instructions."

Kitty tapped Liberty's arm. "Uh, don't look now, Libs, but your handsome co-chair is headed this way."

Liberty glanced over her shoulder, and sleet shot through her veins when she spied Finn breaking free from his crowd of admirers to amble her way. "Tell him I left for the pot-luck," she hissed, pulse pumping as she darted around the booth to enter the back. Before he could make it to their side of the field, Liberty had the makeshift schoolroom doors bolted tight. Her breathing shallowed as she wedged herself deep in the corner.

"Congratulations, ladies, on the win," she heard Finn say, "although I sure hated to lose that prize money." He paused. "Where's Libby?"

"Uh, she l-left for the p-potluck, I think," Kitty lied, the wobble of her voice far from convincing.

"Are you sure?" Finn's tone clearly conveyed his doubt, and Libby squeezed her eyes shut as he continued, barely able to breathe. "Because I could have sworn I saw her over here."

"She w-was, Finn, but she didn't want to be late for the potluck," Martha volunteered in a weak tone.

Kitty's voice rose several octaves. "But we're on our way there now, so why don't we walk over together?"

"Thanks, Kitty, but I'm on my way to help Milo shut down his booth, so I'll see you ladies there, all right?"

"Sure," Kitty and Martha said in unison, and Liberty allowed a slow release of air through her lips. The last thing she wanted was to speak with that womanizing skunk right now, and after dessert at the Poppys' tonight, she planned to never talk to him again.

Waiting in silence for several moments to make sure the coast was clear, Libby tiptoed over to peek out the back door and expelled a silent sigh, satisfied that she was finally alone. Relieved, she slipped out to make her way to the potluck, where at least she could disappear into the crowd.

"Howdy, Libs."

Liberty vaulted at least two inches in the air before she whirled to see Finn butted against the side of their booth, arms in a casual fold.

He delivered a lazy smile. "I thought we decided the potluck would be in the barn."

"Blue blistering blazes, you scared me half to death!" she rasped, hand to her chest as she forced herself to breathe.

His smile faded as sobriety bled into his tone, gaze tender. "And you're scaring me half to death too, darlin', the way you're avoiding me like you are."

Her jaw hardened as she glared right back, not willing to give him a chance to soften her defenses. "I've been busy," she said, spinning on her heel to take her leave.

Finn fell into step beside her, his long legs easily keeping up with her hurried pace. "Yeah, busy avoiding me, and I want to know why."

She yanked her skirts up to quicken her stride, ignoring him and all the curious stares coming their way. "Why don't you ask Jo Beth, you ... you ... wolf in sheep's clothing!"

"Whoa!" He clamped a hand to her wrist to turn her around, latching firm palms to both of her arms. "Where in tarnation did *that* come from?"

"From the lips of a woman you've bamboozled for the last time, Finn McShane, so you can just pack up your sweet talk and peddle it to Jo Beth."

"Now just hold on right there, woman, because we need to talk."

She jerked free, eyes blazing like wildfire. "You mean 'kiss,' don't you, Finn? Because that's how you get your way with all the ladies, isn't it, you two-timing Romeo?" Reloading with another ragged breath, she blasted him with everything she had, taking deadly aim. "Well, I'm done talking or whatever you want to call it. Because you are nothing but a low-down, no-good womanizing varmint, Finn *McShame*, just like your father, cheating and stealing from innocent women before you leave them high and dry."

His face went so pale, she could see the black stubble on his jaw. Her heart lurched at the pain she saw in his eyes and knew she should stop. But all she could see was all the times he'd hurt her over the years and taken advantage whenever it suited his fancy. In the space of one ragged heartbeat, the fire in her belly whooshed out of control and she stepped in to bludgeon his chest with a finger. "My daddy said you were a fortune hunter from the get-go, but I didn't believe him till now, playing one banker's daughter against the other. I didn't trust you growing up, Finn McShane, and I sure don't trust you now. As far as I'm concerned, this is just another one of your pranks to hurt me all over again, and there's nothing you can do or say that will change my mind."

He blinked, the shock in his eyes darkening from hurt into anger. A tic flickered in his cheek as he slowly removed her finger, his manner deadly calm. "Then I guess I best be on my way," he said quietly, leaving a hole in Liberty's chest when he turned and walked away.

"You do that," she shouted, not one bit concerned there were still people milling about. "You go on back to Jo Beth and her daddy's money so you can ruin her life like you just ruined mine."

She slapped at the tears webbing her lashes, wondering why she felt so darn guilty.

"Hey, Libs, where's Finn going in such an all-fire hurry?"

She turned on Milo Parks like a desert dust storm, ready to spew on Finn's best friend like she just had on Finn. Eyes weighting closed, she forced herself to calm down, hand pressed to her stomach to keep from railing on her boss. "I don't know and I don't care," she whispered, as furious over the tears blurring her eyes as she was at Finn.

Cocking a hip, Milo nudged his hat up. "Well, you should, because he sure in the devil cares about you."

"Ha!" She clutched her arms to her waist, thrusting her chin to keep it from trembling. "Finn McShane only cares about two things, Milo Parks, and that's his almighty bank account and breaking women's hearts."

"That so?" Milo matched her stance with a loose fold of arms. "Then suppose you tell me why he didn't win the contest?"

Her jaw notched up several degrees. "The women of this

town finally wised up?"

"Nope." Milo scratched the back of his head, gaze glued to hers. "He withdrew."

She blinked, then blinked again. "I don't believe it. That prize money would go a long way in helping to pay off his almighty loan." She flung an arm towards the V&T steam engine, nose scrunched as if she could still smell that blasted smoke. "He went to all that trouble to dazzle his admirers, so why in blue blazes would he withdraw?"

"I don't know—maybe 'cause he cares more for some hot-headed woman than he does the money? You tell me."

"Prairie Poop!" she shouted, not giving a flip who heard her swear. "Maybe you should ask the woman he plans to marry."

Milo leaned in with a hard gleam in his eyes, hands on his hips. "I-am."

Liberty swallowed hard, hands shaking as she balled them at her sides. "What are you talking about, Milo? He took Jo Beth home from the dance last night, right after he had the nerve to kiss me, when he was planning to propose to her all along."

Milo bent in, practically nose to nose. "Says-who?"

Libby thrust a thumbnail to her mouth, chewing a sliver off before spitting it back out. "Jo Beth, of course. I overheard her tell Bettie that"—Libby plastered a hand over her heart with a toss of her head, mimicking Jo Beth with an exaggerated bat of her eyes—"'I think that gorgeous man is finally going to propose.'" Another splinter of nail sailed through the air

Milo pinched the bridge of his nose, smile flat and tone dry. "Of course."

"Well, he took her home last night, didn't he?" Liberty countered with a purse of her lips, "and Nellie Sue told Kristi Lemp that Finn came in to buy Jo Beth a wedding ring just two weeks ago." Liberty crossed her arms with great drama, her anger helping to temper some of her hurt.

"So how do you answer that?"

Milo gave a slow nod. "Yes, he took Jo Beth home last night because it was her birthday and he promised to celebrate it with her and her family months ago."

Pthu! Another shred of nail shot into the air. "Well, smarty-pants, how do you explain the wedding ring, then?" she challenged, staunch in her efforts to keep any and all tears at bay.

Milo shook his head, lips skewed in disbelief. "You know, Liberty, you may have been valedictorian at Vassar, but when it comes to love, you can be pretty darn stupid." He angled in, gaze sharp as he gave full vent to a scowl. "He bought a ring all right, Miss O'Shea, but not for Jo Beth."

A cold chill chased all blood from her face. She gulped. "F-for who, then?"

"For *you*, you mule-headed woman. Blue blazes, Liberty—I didn't even know the man liked you, much less planned to marry you! May as well whopped me with a dad-burned two-ton press—couldn't have stunned me more. Told me just this morning he planned to propose after he paid off his loan, which if Jo Beth finds out he broke it off with her this morning to take up with you, may take a whole lot longer than he hoped."

An odd mix of joy and grief rolled in her stomach. "He … he broke it off with Jo Beth?"

Milo's lips took a twist. "Don't know if they taught you this in that fancy school of yours, Libs, but bigamy is frowned upon in these here parts."

Liberty cupped hands to her mouth, heart suddenly light as air. "He wasn't lying to me, then …"

"Uh, no, because contrary to your long-held beliefs, the man is rather partial to the truth."

The truth. Liberty gasped. "Oh, no!" She peered up at Milo with frantic eyes. "I said awful things to him, Milo, hateful things about both him and his father."

A low groan slipped from Milo's lips. "Sweet soul-saving mercy, Liberty, the man has spent his entire life trying to be everything his father wasn't, desperate to erase the damage done to both his family and his name. And you throw it all in his face?"

"I ... I didn't know ..." she whispered, heart aching over the damage she'd done.

"Well you do now, woman, so you need to fix it. But I'm warning you—it won't be easy. I've been Finn's best friend since we've been crawling in cow pastures, and the one time I compared him to his old man, he didn't talk to me for nigh on three months."

"But he finally did, right?" Liberty cast him a hopeful look.

Milo turned away to tunnel fingers through his hair, shaking his head with a low chuckle. "Yeah, he finally did, but not without a whole lot of fancy finagling, I can tell you that."

A slow grin eased across Liberty's face. "I can finagle," she said with a chew of her lip, "and I smell a whole lot better than you."

His laughter rang out as he looped an arm to her shoulders. "That you do, Libs, and you can light a fire under that boy faster than anybody I've ever seen. But I'll tell you what, Miss O'Shea, when you two finally *do* get together?" He gave her a wink while he ushered her to the barn, shaking his head along the way. "It'll be Fourth of July every bloomin' day of the year."

CHAPTER TWENTY-ONE

"FINN—YOU'RE EARLY!" MRS. POPPY PUSHED the screen open, her smile as wide as the door she held, inviting him into a house that smelled like cinnamon sticks and lemons. Despite his frustrated mood, his mouth instantly watered for a slice of her prize-winning cake. Her pink cheeks puffed with pleasure as she waved him in, the signature silver topknot bouncing as she bustled down the hall. "Are the fireworks over already?"

They are for me. He forced a smile as she glanced his way, determined to curtail his nasty mood with the two people in his life who deserved it the least. "Naw, they just started, lighting up that new town square like high noon, so I imagine it'll be a while." He peered into the parlour as he followed her, Stetson in hand. "Is the pastor around?"

Her usual sparkle dimmed as she led him into the cozy kitchen where her table was all dressed up with her best lace tablecloth and a pitcher of poppies. Two candles flickered in anticipation of company, along with her antique oil lamp, which due to the crimp in her brow, now glowed far more than its hostess. "Why, yes, of course, Finn. I just sent him out to the garden to fetch some peppermint for our tea." She placed a gentle hand on his arm. "Is something … wrong?"

Everything. "No, ma'am, nothing to fret about. I'm just looking for a piece of advice from both you and the pastor."

"I see." It was clear from the gentle slope of silver brows that she did see, most likely, reading his mind as if she were blood. *And they may as well be.* Pastor Poppy had stepped in as a father figure when Finn's own father had abandoned him, teaching him how to be the man he so wanted to be. No telling where he'd be today without the Poppys' influence and rock-solid faith. A faith that had not only saved his sorry soul, but his life as well, guiding him, teaching him.

Redeeming him.

And literally saving him from a fate worse than death.

Becoming my father's son.

Finn paused to put a hand to his eyes. The pain of Libby's attack was still brutally fresh, despite the half cord of wood he split on his land in record time during the potluck and talent show. Those had been Libby's responsibilities for the festival, so he knew he wouldn't be missed.

Especially by her.

But every crack of the ax had splintered the wood like her words had splintered his soul, convincing him that no matter how much he wanted her, they were no good for each other. She was a bolt of lightening to the solid and secure timber of his life, a life he had built from the ground up after his father had destroyed both his hope and his family. Yes, she electrified him with her passion and purpose like no other woman ever had. But somehow she always left smoldering ruins in her wake, singeing his temper like no one else ever could.

Like tonight.

Comparing him to his father had unleashed a fury so strong, his first thought was to douse his temper with that 80-proof rotgut they served at the Brass Rail. He unleashed a grunt. Some called it "coffin varnish," and they weren't far wrong, but Finn hadn't had an urge to partake for over two years now since the Poppys had given him a reason not to. That is, until the woman whose love and respect he craved kicked him in the gut.

"You are nothing but a low-down, no-good womanizing varmint just like your father, Finn McShane, cheating and stealing from innocent women before you leave them high and dry."

Talk about coffin varnish!

"Finn."

He glanced up, startled that he'd obviously drifted off given the steaming cup Mrs. Poppy had set at his usual place at the table. She patted the back of his chair with a tender look. "You sit right here with a cup of my special poppy-seed tea—it'll calm you, son. I'll go get Horace, all right?" She squeezed his shoulder when he sat down, her gentle touch as comforting as her tea.

How many cups had he consumed right here at this table over the last few years, he wondered, soothing his body as much as the Poppys' faith had soothed his soul. Too many to count, he knew, and yet never was there a more critical time than tonight.

"Finn, my boy!" Pastor Poppy held the door for his wife when they entered the kitchen a few moments later, the smile on his face unable to mask the concern in his eyes. "We weren't expecting you and Liberty for another hour or so."

Finn rose and nodded. "Yes, sir, but I'm in need of some advice from the two smartest people I know, so I hope you don't mind that I came early?"

"Oh, pish-posh!" Mrs. Poppy said with a wave of her hand, hurrying over to pour cups of tea for the pastor and herself. "You are welcome here anytime, any day, Griffin McShane, and well you know it. Now, sit and tell us what's put that frown on your face?"

Finn took a sip of his tea and set it back down, peering up beneath beetled brows. "It's Liberty."

"Why, of course it is, you sweet boy," Mrs. Poppy said with a gentle pat on his back. "You're in love with her, for heaven's sake, so naturally you're going to be out of sorts until you up and marry the girl."

She may as well have knocked him back in the chair—he gaped all the same. "Holy thunder, ma'am, sometimes I think you are out-and-out clairvoyant, how you see things nobody else can see."

Her lips pursed in a knowing smile. "You mean like the disdain you pretend to have for Liberty when all the time you're lovesick to the core?" She dismissed the notion with a wave of her hand. "I wasn't born yesterday, Griffin McShane, so you can't fool me. I see straight through your bickering to how much you care for the girl, for heaven's sake."

"That's just it, ma'am," he said with another quick gulp of tea, "I'm not so sure it's 'for heaven's sake.'"

Pastor Poppy leaned in with a squint. "Why do you say that, Finn? You were as high as a hog in a halo after you and I talked privately this morning, determined to end it with Jo Beth no matter the risk to you or your loan."

Finn nodded slowly. "Yes, sir, I was, and I took it to heart when you said 'true liberty is doing the right thing,' even planning to propose to Liberty tonight with the rings that I bought."

The old man nodded slowly, a faint smile shadowing his lips. "If the Son therefore shall make you free, ye shall be *free indeed.*"

"*And* free to marry the right woman," Mrs. Poppy added, the sparkle back in her eyes.

Finn cuffed the back of his neck, gaze sober. "Yes, ma'am, but right at this moment, I'm not so sure Libby is the right woman, least not after the awful things she said to me this morning."

"All couples say awful things when they're angry, isn't that so, Horace?"

Mr. Poppy studied Finn with a keen eye. "Yes, yes that's true, Clara." His gaze sharpened. "But I suspect this may go deeper than a few angry words, eh, Finn?"

Finn expelled a weary sigh. "Yes, sir, it does, at least for me. You see Liberty said some pretty hateful things to me this morning, and I have no earthly reason why. Wouldn't explain, just fired me up hotter than those red-hot Roman candles shooting up out of town square." He kneaded the bridge of his nose with another heavy expulsion of air. "Haven't lost my temper like that in a long, long while." A shudder rippled through him. "Actually thought about going to the Brass Rail if you can believe that, which made me feel so low, so worthless, so much like …" His voice tapered off as muscles constricted in his throat.

"Your pa?" The compassion in Pastor Poppy's voice caused moisture to sting at the back of Finn's lids.

"Yeah," he said quietly, shocked at just how much the thought scared the living daylights out of him. That Liberty could trigger that.

Which meant, suddenly she scared the daylights out of him too.

"What if I'm no good for her?" He glanced up, a dull ache in his chest as he stared at the pastor. "What if she's no good for me? I mean nobody lights my temper up like that woman, and yet no one lights my life up like her either. But when she said what she did, compared me to my pa like that, it just got me to thinking, you know? About how we're always butting heads about one thing or another and I … I just don't know, Pastor." He trailed into a vacant stare. "I don't know if my love is strong enough to handle that."

"You're afraid," Pastor Poppy confirmed softly.

Finn's gaze jerked back, eyes wide. "You're darn right I am, sir. Scared silly if you want to know, that we'll wind up in a marriage where we end up hating each other."

"Just like your folks." Mrs. Poppy's quiet statement met its mark, piercing Finn's heart with a fear he'd never acknowledged before.

"Yeah," he whispered, eyes lagging into another ten-mile

stare. "Just like them."

"You know, Finn ..." The pastor paused. "Perfect love casts out fear."

Finn cut loose with a grunt. "Yeah, well, our love is anything but perfect, sir." He upended his tea.

"No ... but God's love is, and where the Spirit of the Lord is, there is *liberty.*"

Finn's brows jabbed low. "Pardon me, sir, but is that an oxymoron?"

Pastor Poppy laughed. "Not really," he said with a pensive scratch at the nape of his neck. "Although I'm sure it sounds like it right about now." He refocused on Finn with a probing stare. "It just means you're a man of God now, Finn, and not in this alone anymore. You have God's Spirit, His precepts, and His grace to help you do the right thing." His mouth quirked. "Even *when* you do the wrong thing like lose your temper."

Finn stared, the truth of God's Word warming his spirit like Mrs. Poppy's tea warmed his soul. "True liberty," he whispered, the barest spark of hope flickering in his chest.

"Yep." Pastor Poppy raised his cup in a toast. "The kind that helps you love a human being no matter their frailties *or* your own."

"*Or* a hot-tempered woman," Mrs. Poppy said with a giggle.

"You mean a hot-tempered little brat." Finn slid the old woman a sliver of a smile.

"Whom you have forgiven, yes?" Pastor Poppy's brow angled high.

"Not yet, but I will." Finn's mouth took a slant. "Eventually." He issued a grunt. "Although I won't make it easy for her, sir, I can promise you that. Liberty O'Shea needs to learn to mind her mouth and her temper, and I'm just the man to teach her." Huffing out a noisy sigh, he slashed his fingers through his hair. "Pardon my irritation, Pastor, but right now I'm still a little gun-shy as far as that woman is concerned."

"Perfectly understandable," Pastor Poppy said with a thoughtful nod. "In fact, given your concerns, it might be wise to slow the entire process down. You know, wait until you've paid off that loan before you make a decision about courting, like you originally planned to do."

The edge of Finn's mouth kicked up. "Which might be a lot longer than I thought given the lemonade Jo Beth threw in my face."

"Oh my, I bet that put *both* of you in a sour mood," Mrs. Poppy said with a giggle.

Pastor Poppy smiled as he stirred more sugar into his tea. "No doubt about that, Clara. But you know what I mean, Finn—take time to get to know Liberty a little better. Then let God make the decision for you."

Finn ducked his head, eyes in a squint. "Pardon me?"

The pastor chuckled. "I mean we'll pray about it, of course, but then let nature take its course"—he winked— "and God."

Finn's curious gaze flicked from Pastor Poppy to his wife and back. "'Nature' taking its course I can understand, sir, but I'm not exactly sure how that will help me know what God wants me to do."

"Oh, you'll know," Mrs. Poppy said with a laugh, glancing at the watch pinned to her bodice before she jumped up to pull dessert plates from the cupboard. "Because the Lord may speak in a still small voice, Griffin McShane, but trust me." She tossed him a smile while she put the tea back on the boil. "The impact is deafening."

CHAPTER TWENTY-TWO

LEGS AS WOBBLY AS HER stomach, Liberty smoothed her skirt with sweaty hands as she stood on the Poppys' front porch, finally mustering the courage to knock on their screen door. "Please don't let him hate me," she whispered, pretty sure Finn had changed his mind about ever courting a hothead like her.

"Liberty, hello! And, goodness, you're early too." Mrs. Poppy scuttled down the hall from the kitchen, where a light glowed like the woman before her. She giggled. "As was Finn, so it must be my prize-winning cake that lured you both in."

"Without question," Liberty said with a shy smile. *That and the handsome young man eating it with me.* She cast a nervous glance at Finn's horse who chewed on clover next to the front porch, then slipped through the screen door Mrs. Poppy held open, her heart beating a little too fast to suit. The *same* handsome young man she hadn't seen since she'd lambasted him earlier in the day.

"Well, I baked a special cake especially for you and Finn, I'll have you know, just to say thank you for all the hard work you both put in for our fair town." She shot a grin over her shoulder as she hurried down the hall. "Our co-chairs deserve it warm, right out of the oven—*with* ice cream!" She tugged Liberty into the kitchen that always seemed so welcoming with its eyelet curtains fluttering in the breeze and cast-iron stove bubbling with wonderful smells. Liberty peeked at Finn, and the hard clamp of his mouth twisted her stomach. Welcoming, yes.

Except for tonight.

"Look who I found out on the front porch," Mrs. Poppy said with a husky chuckle, "the prettiest co-chair of the bunch."

"No argument there," Finn said with a hard smile as he slowly rose from the table.

Mrs. Poppy steered Liberty to the chair right next to Finn's and nudged her down. "Now, you sit right here, young lady, and I'll fix you a calming cup of poppy-seed tea to go with my special lemon-mint poppy-seed cake, all right?"

"Thank you, ma'am," Liberty whispered, not daring to look Finn's way.

"Liberty, congratulations to you and Finn for a job well-done on the best festival our town has ever had." Pastor Poppy retrieved dessert plates laden with napkins and utensils from the counter while his wife poured Liberty a fresh cup of tea.

Jumping up to assist, Liberty took the plates from him to distribute with shaky hands, well aware of Finn's cool stare boring a hole right through her. "Thank you, Pastor Poppy, but we certainly couldn't have done it without you and Mrs. Poppy, that's for sure, so the lion's share of the thanks goes to both of you."

"So tell me, Liberty and Finn," Mrs. Poppy said, pulling potholders out of a drawer with a smile a whole lot warmer than the one on Finn's face, "now that the festival's almost over, I'll bet you two are going to miss working so closely together, aren't you?"

"Doubt it." Finn's sullen response was so low, Liberty knew it was for her benefit alone.

"Believe it or not, ma'am," Liberty said slowly, sneaking a peek Finn's way, "I will miss working with Mr. McShane because he was always such a ..."—a hint of mischief twitched on her lips—"challenge."

"*Me?*" Finn leaned in to sear her with a look.

Liberty couldn't resist a tiny smile while she nibbled the edge of her lip. "As I'm sure you already know, he can be pretty ... stubborn."

"Ha! That's the jackass calling the donkey a mule if ever there was."

Mrs. Poppy's laughter floated through the air along with the smell of fresh-baked poppy-seed cake as she pulled it out of the oven. "Yes, I do believe the pastor and I can attest to seeing a bit of the mule here and there over the years."

"Here and there?" Liberty's brows shot high as she put a hand to her mouth to shield a giggle. "Goodness, Mrs. Poppy, when I leave our meetings, I literally fall into bed because the man plumb wears me out."

"Uh, that would be from all your yammering, Miss O'Shea, which I can attest saps every ounce of energy I have."

Liberty slid him a shy peek, cheeks suddenly warm. "Well, maybe not *all* your energy ..."

"Here we go ..." Potholders in hand, Mrs. Poppy delivered the cake to the table. The heavenly smell rumbled Liberty's stomach, an unwelcome reminder she'd had no appetite at the potluck. "Hot out of the oven!" She proceeded to cut healthy pieces and slather them with glazed icing that watered Liberty's mouth.

One bite and Liberty almost moaned, eyelids drifting closed while she savored the best cake she'd ever tasted.

"Clara, you've outdone yourself tonight, dear." Pastor Poppy tucked into the dessert with gusto, a contented smile spanning his face. "I do believe this is your best yet."

"I have to agree, Mrs. Poppy," Finn said, licking the icing off of his fork. And I like the addition of the icing, ma'am, almost better than your original recipe.

"Oh, drat!" Mrs. Poppy sprang up from the table.

Finn's face fell as he blinked at the older woman. "Uh … don't get me wrong, ma'am. I like your original recipe a lot, too, and so does everyone else, apparently, since you win every year."

"Oh, no, no, no!" Mrs. Poppy pushed her chair in with a pointed look at her husband before bestowing a sweet smile on Finn. "I'm not offended that you like this version better, Finn," she explained, "I just remembered Horace forgot to bring in the mint for our tea and I forgot about the ice cream I made especially for tonight." Hurrying over to pump more water into the teapot, she put it back on the boil, then plucked an empty mason jar off her counter along with a lantern. She returned to where her husband was helping himself to a second piece of cake. "Your stomach can wait, Horace—but our tea and ice cream cannot." Tugging him up with an apologetic smile at Libby that didn't quite ring true, she handed him the lantern with a nod toward the door. "Liberty, Finn—please forgive us, but we'll be right back, so you two just go ahead and visit a while, all right?"

No! Finn launched to his feet like a blasted Chinese sky-rocket, chair clattering loudly against the wooden planks of the floor. He was pretty darn sure what Mrs. Poppy had up her sleeve, but he wasn't ready. Not yet. The last thing he wanted was to hob-knob with Liberty O'Shea right now, not with this splinter of hurt still festering in his heart. He shoved his chair in and strode to the door, swiping the jar right out of her hand. "No, let me gather the peppermint for you, ma'am, while you and the pastor stay and visit with your guest."

A shadow of a smile twitched on the old woman's lips as she snatched the jar back, silver brows spiking high. "Tell me, Finn—do you even know what peppermint looks like?"

He swallowed hard, heat ringing his collar. "Uh no, ma'am, but all I have to do is pinch the leaves and smell it, right?"

Smile maternal, Mrs. Poppy patted Finn's cheek with a look of affection, but the suspicious twinkle in her gaze told him he was a goner. "Thank you, you sweet boy, but Mr. Poppy and I have trouble finding it in the dark ourselves, much less sending someone who doesn't know where it is in my huge garden *or* how to pick it the way I like."

Pastor Poppy slapped Finn on the shoulder with a chuckle. "Give it up, Finn, you won't win, trust me. I've been trying for over fifty years, son, so I'd advise you to just sit down and enjoy more cake."

The screen slammed, and Finn just stared out the door for several painful seconds, unwilling to turn around lest he lose some of his anger. And he couldn't afford to. Oh, he had every intention of eventually courting Liberty if God directed him that way, but *not* before he made his point. The woman he married needed to know the full meaning of the Scripture, "the tongue is a fire," and Finn figured a bit of cold shoulder and time would go a long way in educating her. Liberty was a feisty, headstrong little thing who could sure set him on fire—both temper *and* body—and he wasn't about to give her the chance to do either right now. His mouth thinned with resolve.

Inside of marriage or not.

Because as much as he loved his mother, he vowed he'd never allow a woman to trip his temper like she had with his father, always nagging and butting heads over every little thing. That didn't absolve his father from drinking, infidelity, and abandonment, certainly, but deep down Finn couldn't help but believe it was a factor in the destruction of their marriage. And he'd be horsewhipped and hung up to dry before he'd *ever* let that happen to him.

Without a word, he opted for a chair across the table

from Liberty instead of next to her like before and immediately reached for the cake. Cutting a piece, he glanced
up with a tight pinch of lips, one brow jagging high as he
extended the cake her way.

"Please," she said quietly, pushing her plate forward so
he could serve her. "I suspect this is next year's winner for
sure." Rising, she offered a tiny smile, contrition soft in her
eyes. "I could use more tea. How 'bout you?"

He gave an abrupt nod and sliced another section for
himself while she retrieved the teapot. Ignoring her as
she poured, he shoveled more cake in his mouth, staring
straight ahead while he chewed.

"Finn ..." Her whispered plea matched the gentle touch
of her hand on his shoulder, paralyzing him mid-chew.
"Will you forgive me—please?"

His eyelids weighted closed as he swallowed, the scent of
lilacs leaching his anger. Laying his fork down, he pushed
away from the table with a stiff fold of arms. "Of course
I forgive you, Libby, but what you said"—he peered up
at her, wondering how he could both love and hate the
fire she possessed—"it wounded me to the core, and to
be honest, I'm not all that sure we're right for each other."

A muscle spasmed in her throat, and he fought the urge
to jump up and take her in his arms. But he couldn't. Not
yet.

This was way too important.

She rounded the table to pour her own tea, then returned
the teapot before she sagged into her chair, eyes fixed on
the cup in her hands. "I deserve that, of course, and I apologize for losing my temper and for what I said, but"—she
glanced up, a bit of the fire back in her eyes—"you could
have told me you broke it off with Jo Beth."

He cocked a brow. "Would you have believed me?"

Her chest rose and fell in a shaky sigh as she caught the
edge of her lip with her teeth.

"I didn't think so." The twitch in his temple told him his

anger was alive and well as he took a glug of his tea, cup wobbling in the saucer when he slammed it back down. "So instead of talking it out with me, you go for the throat, Libby, with a tongue as sharp as a bowie knife, gutting me to the core."

She had the grace to blush.

He leaned in, desperate to make her understand.

Desperate to make it work.

"Libby, I want you more than I've ever wanted any woman, but my parents fought like two cocks in a cage, drawing blood every single time. They sliced each other up with their words and actions until my father ran off with another woman, leaving our family in shreds." Drawing in a deep gulp of air, he slowly straightened, some of his frustration seeping out in a lumbering sigh. "And frankly, Libs, I don't want that for myself, and I sure don't want that for us."

"Me either, Finn," she whispered, green eyes moist with regret.

Her tears dismantled more of his anger, and upending his tea, a calm settled over him as he reclaimed the seat beside her. "Libby," he said quietly, taking her hand in his, "I love you, I do, but I think we both need to step back and take some time. You know, to pray about it and make sure we're a good fit."

She peeked up beneath dark lashes spiked with tears, and he smothered a groan, heat spiraling through his belly when he glanced at those pink lips, moist with invitation. "I don't think the 'fit' is the problem, Finn," she said softly, a pretty blush dusting her cheeks as her gaze dropped to his mouth.

He quickly distanced himself several inches with a loud screech of his chair, not about to let feminine wiles railroad him into moving too fast. He gulped more tea. No matter *how* potent those blasted wiles might be.

Liberty scooted closer, eyes soft with affection. "I love

you, too, Finn, and I promise to work on my temper—"

"Good," he said with a gruff clear of his throat, his heart already on the thaw.

"If you work on yours …"

His jaw dropped. "*Mine?*" He shot up, more steam coming out of his ears than Mrs. Poppy's teapot on full boil. Blue blazes, it was his poor excuse for a father who had the temper—not him, and nothing made Finn want to spit fire more than that blasted comparison. Not when he'd spent a lifetime trying to purge it from his mind. Holy thunder, he hadn't even realized he still *had* a blasted temper till she came back to town. He jumped up to storm over to the stove, suddenly craving a whole pot of Mrs. Poppy's tea. "You mean the temper I don't have unless *you* trigger it?"

"Yes, *that* temper," she emphasized, nodding her thanks when he topped off her cup. "Goodness, my temper wouldn't even be a problem if you weren't such a bully."

"Me?" Finn gaped as he banged the teapot back onto the stove, marching back to stare her down with hands moored low on his hips. "I wouldn't be a bully if you weren't so pushy in the first place, Miss Bell, always wrestling for control."

Liberty blasted from her seat to glare right back, ramming a petite finger against his chest for good measure. "And I wouldn't have to wrestle for control in the first place if you'd just treat me with the same courtesy and respect you do with a man, giving ear to my ideas instead of dismissing me as a mere woman."

Finn couldn't help it—he grinned, her fire never failing to disarm and lure him in. "But that's just it, Libs," he said softly, his gaze straying to her mouth as he took hold of her wrist, "you're *not* a man, and I have never been happier of anything more in my life. And heaven knows you are *definitely* no mere woman." He slowly reeled her in, eyelids shuttering closed as he bent to give her way more than an ear.

Oooomph! Two tiny palms slammed against his chest, jolting his eyes open. "Hold it right there, buster!" she said with a no-nonsense glint in her eyes, "you are not sidetracking me this time, Finn McShane. We have serious problems here, mister, and we need to resolve them."

Huffing out a groaning sigh, Finn gouged stiff fingers through his hair. "Fine, you're right—we *do* need to resolve our differences. And, yes, I will admit that as much as I squawked about it, you had some pretty good ideas for making the festival a success. So you have my word that I will *try* to keep more of an open mind where you and your opinions are concerned."

"Thank you," she said in a considerably less agitated tone as her palms finally relaxed against his chest, their slow slide down his shirt leaving a trail of fire in their wake. "And I will *try* to rein in both my temper and my tongue *if* you work on being less of a bully."

His mouth crooked as he slipped an arm to her waist, drawing her close once again. "Agreed if *you* work on being less pushy and demanding—"

"Demanding?!" Her body stiffened as she attempted to push him away once more. "I'll give you 'demanding,' you mule-headed—"

Her protest faded into his mouth as he jerked her close and kissed her hard, the taste of Libby O'Shea far better than any award-winning cake. He buried his head in her neck with a loud groan. "Libby, I love you—*why* are we fighting?"

He felt the shift of her throat as she swallowed, her breathing as shallow as his. "Because we're so good at it?" Her voice was a breathless rasp.

"We are, no question, sweetheart, but we are *so* much better at this …" He nuzzled her earlobe before skimming his mouth back to hers, their moans merging when he deepened the kiss.

"*Ahem* …" The gruff clear of a throat blasted them apart

like a stick of dynamite.

Heat roared into Finn's cheeks as he further distanced himself from Libby with several additional steps back, the knowing smile on Pastor Poppy's face doing nothing for Finn's composure. "Uh, pardon us, sir, but we were just discussing our future together."

"I see," he said with a wink at Libby that only served to deepen the bloom in her cheeks. Chuckling, he set the lamp on the counter along with a crock of ice cream while Mrs. Poppy rinsed off the mint from her mason jar, the smiles on their faces prompting the same on Finn's. "A good discussion, was it?"

Finn glanced at Libby, who nibbled the edge of her lip while her face flamed near as bright as her hair. He grinned. "Yes, sir, it was, although we definitely have some work ahead of us."

Mrs. Poppy dropped several mint leaves into her tea-pot, her face beaming like the full moon out the kitchen window. "Oh my, I am *so* excited! I've had a feeling about you two youngsters from the very start, so I am delighted to hear you've worked things out." She slapped her palms together in prayer mode, eyes sparkling more than the candlelight flickering in their tea. "So … you've decided to court?"

Finn's gaze collided with Libby's, and he grinned ear to ear. "I think that's safe to say, ma'am, although we do plan to take it slow."

The pastor's laughter filled the cozy kitchen as he took his seat, diving back into his cake without missing a beat. "Any slower, my boy, and you two could be married by morning."

Finn blinked. It was a contest over which generated more heat—his neck or Libby's face.

"Now, Horace, hush—you're embarrassing our guests." Mrs. Poppy offered a conciliatory smile while she doled out more cake. A soft gasp popped from her mouth. "Oh my stars—I almost forgot about the ice cream—*again!*"

Retrieving a scoop from a drawer, she quickly delivered the crock to the table with a proud lift of her chin. "The perfect treat to celebrate a courtship! And, I'll have you know, made with special poppy seeds all the way from Spain, sent by Horace's missionary friend." Her brow wrinkled the slightest bit. "Of course, I almost ruined it when I dropped the whole silly bottle into the mix, but I tasted it, and it really has a lovely little crunch to it, so I hope you like it too." Her face broke into a bright smile that chased all the worry lines away. "So tell me, Finn," she asked as she plopped a large spoonful of ice cream onto his cake, "are you going to ask Libby's father for permission to court her?"

"Yes—"

"No!" Libby quickly interrupted, smiling her thanks when Mrs. Poppy topped her cake with ice cream. "If it's all the same to you and the pastor, Mrs. Poppy, we'd rather keep it quiet for a while for a number of reasons."

"*What?*" Finn almost choked on the ice cream he'd just shoveled in, lunging for his tea when he began to hack.

"As you know, my father has never been overly"—she sent Finn a feeble smile—"fond of Finn, so I think it's best if we just lay low for a while—"

"Lay low?" Finn's jaw practically came unhinged. "Now look here, Libby, there's no way I'm going to court you behind your father's back—"

"It's just for a while, Finn," Libby pleaded, "till I can ease him in slowly that you and I have fallen in love. Besides, you said it yourself—it will give Jo Beth time to adjust and you time to pay off your loan."

Finn began to grind his jaw, pretty sure Libby was right, but not one bit happy about it. When he'd been angry with her, waiting had seemed like a viable option, but now that he knew he wanted to marry her and she wanted to marry him, he just wanted to get on with their lives and the loan be hung. "We tell your father and everyone else by August 1ˢᵗ then."

Libby was shaking her head before he'd uttered his final word. "I really think we need to wait longer, Finn, at least three months."

He bounded up. "Three months! Confound it, Libby, I love you, and I don't want to wait."

She rose and took his hands in hers, eyes gentle. "And I love you, too, but it will give you more time to accomplish all we need to do—prepare my father for the news, ease Jo Beth's heartache, pay off your loan …" She lifted on tiptoe to brush a soft kiss to his cheek. "Ready your cabin for a wife …" Her eyes sparkled with promise and tease. "*Plus* more time to see if you and I are a 'good fit.'"

It took everything in him not to haul her back into his arms and prove the fit was plum perfect. Unleashing a weary sigh, he kissed her nose instead. "All right, Miss O'Shea—you win." He arched a brow. "This round, that is. But ready or not, come October 1ˢᵗ, I plan to court you true and proper in front of God and everybody, understood?"

"Yessss, Mr. *McPain*," Libby said in a sing-song tone while she sat back down to sample her ice cream.

Finn tweaked the back of her neck, prompting a giggle from her lips as he joined her. "I wouldn't be making too much fun of that name, darlin', because if I have my way, you'll be wearing it for a long time to come."

"Oh, I just love weddings!" Mrs. Poppy clapped her hands, her manner almost giddy. Picking her spoon back up she sent Finn a wink, obviously ready to begin the celebration with ice cream and cake. "And three months may seem like a lifetime now, but you mark my words, young man," she said with a wiggle of brows, "I have a feeling it will go by in a blink."

CHAPTER TWENTY-THREE

*B*LINK. LIBERTY SQUINTED THROUGH SLEEPY eyes, near blinded by the sunshine washing her bedroom with its glorious light. *Mmm … what a wonderful dream*, she thought with a lazy stretch in her bed, eyelids sinking closed as memories of Finn's kisses heated her body more than the shaft of daylight warming her skin.

It was official—Finn wanted to court her, and although it would be her father's worst nightmare—which he'd surely fight till the end—for Liberty, it was a life-long dream come true.

Mrs. Griffin McShane.

A dreamy sigh wisped across her lips as she replayed last night at the Poppys'. Yes, they had some issues to work out, certainly, but this was the man she had pined for since the age of twelve, and Liberty had never been surer of anything in her life.

Breathing in the crisp morning air, she reveled in the heady scent of leather and lime as more memories fluttered her stomach. Besides, keeping their relationship secret for three months would be fun, she'd argued last night, as long as they could still meet to wrap up festival business and propose a plan for next year. A slow smile wended its way across her lips as she thought of the possibilities. Innocent meetings that would benefit both the city and them, affording valuable time to iron out any kinks in their relationship. With another languid stretch, she turned on her side.

After all—what could possibly go wrong?

A strong arm looped her waist, dragging her close. "Mmm ... mornin', darlin'."

Libby froze before she screamed and vaulted from the bed, body shaking while she snatched the sheet off of Finn McShane. "Sweet m-mother of mercy," she rasped, body woozy and mind even worse, "what are you doing here?"

Bleary-eyed beneath a haphazard quilt, Finn lumbered up with a hand to his head. "What the—" Rubbing his eyes, he blinked up at Libby, groggy gaze spanning wide at her state of undress. His face leached as pale as the sheet she clutched to her chest. "Blue blistering blazes ... it's not a dream!" he whispered in a hoarse morning voice as rough as the dark stubble shadowing his jaw. His Adam's apple ducked hard while his gaze wandered from her disheveled hair spilling over bare shoulders down to her bare legs and back up, his grin growing along with the whites of his eyes.

Libby faltered back, fingers quivering as she clutched the sheet around her body. Her gaze darted frantically around the room. "And this isn't my room—it must be the Poppys' guest room, so what on earth happened, Finn?" Her throat convulsed as she stared, cheeks on fire while she wagged a trembling finger between them. "Oh, sweet mother of mercy, we didn't ... did we?"

Finn lumbered up to sag against the headboard, muscled chest bare and eyes closed while he kneaded the bridge of his nose. "Well, it sure seems like we did in my dream, darlin'"—he lowered his fingers to stare at his left hand where a wedding band gleamed bright in the morning sun. Glancing up, he managed a wince of a smile—"so maybe so?"

Her hands flew to her mouth in horror, belly quivering at the thought she'd just spent the night with Finn McShane. "Holy heavenly host—what are we going to do?"

He scooted to the edge of the bed with a sheepish smile,

wrapping the quilt around his middle before tugging her to sit on his lap. "Well, for starters," he whispered, voice husky while he lifted her hand to graze the wedding band on her finger, "I'm going to kiss my wife." And before Liberty could utter a single word, he disarmed her with a playful tug of her lip while slowly easing her back on the bed, devouring her with a kiss that swirled a dangerous heat in her middle. "Great day in the morning, but I love you Mrs. Liberty Margaret McShane, and Mrs. Poppy was right—that three months did go by in a blink."

Liberty gaped, confusion fluttering her lashes as much as Finn's kiss fluttered her stomach. "But ... but ... I don't understand—how did this happen?"

Chuckling, he settled back against the headboard again, hooking her close to his side while he feathered the strands of her hair with his fingers. "Not exactly sure, Libs, but I have a sneakin' suspicion an excessive amount of poppy seeds may have been involved."

Liberty spun around to face him, eyes wide. "Oh my goodness, that's it! I remember reading an article at Vassar once, about certain poppies that are harvested for opium, and I think it said poppy seeds from Spain were particularly powerful."

"Which is why I dreamed Pastor Poppy married us last night, darlin'." The edge of his lips crooked while he lightly traced the line of her bare shoulder with his fingers. "No wonder Mrs. Poppy wins the baking contest every year." His smile faded to soft as he nuzzled her mouth. "Are you sorry, Libs?" he whispered, skimming her jaw to gently suckle the soft flesh of her ear.

A tiny moan escaped as her eyelids drifted closed, the prospect of being Finn's wife suddenly feeling so right. Memories of his tenderness last night, his kisses, his love-making purled through her brain, potent and strong, and her breathing shallowed. She opened her eyes to cup his bristled cheek. "No, Finn, I'm not. Somehow I feel ...

well, like I've been set free, you know? As if I'm ready to embark on a new adventure where I can be the woman I've always dreamed I could be."

A twinkle lit in his eyes as he teased her lip with another tug of his teeth. "My wife?"

"Finn McShane!" She attempted to wrestle him away, but he only laughed, pinning her to the bed with a perilous gleam in his eyes. "But the smartest, prettiest, feistiest wife any man ever had." He lowered to kiss her long and slow before rolling to his side and pulling her along. Buffing her arm, he pressed a kiss to her hair. "The truth is that I feel freer too, Libs, like all this time I've just been waiting for my life to start—with you."

Tap-Tap-Tap. "Uh ... Libby darling, Finn ..." Mrs. Poppy's loud whisper was laced with concern. "It seems we have a slight problem ..."

Finn grinned as he buried his lips in her neck. "Not from where I'm lying," he said softly, drawing her body flush with his.

"Me either ..." Libby's voice was breathless, her tummy tumbling along with her heart.

"*Liberty Margaret O'Shea*—you come down here this instant!"

Libby jolted straight up in the bed, the sound of her father's shout causing her stomach to swoop in a whole 'nother way. "Uh-oh." She gulped, voice shaky. "Uh, please tell Papa we'll be right down, Mrs. Poppy."

"Certainly, dear."

"Oh, and ma'am?" Finn called with a grin, giving Libby a wink. "Dish him up some of that poppy-seed ice cream with a big ol' piece of your famous cake, if you will, along with a nice, big cup of your tea." He eased Libby over on her back with a wicked smile. "Because I have something to say to my wife first"—his voice lowered to husky as he skimmed her throat with his mouth—"and do."

Libby's contented sigh met his when he kissed his way

back up to capture her lips with his own. "Happy Independence Day, Mrs. McShane," he whispered against her skin, "because we're finally free to start our life together. Although I'm pretty sure the fireworks display today won't compare to those we saw last night."

Libby's cheeks warmed along with her body. "That was yesterday, Mr. McShane," she said with a dreamy smile, "today is the 5th of July."

Finn deposited a kiss to her nose, then headed south to nuzzle the curve of her neck. "That may be true, darlin'," he said with a chuckle, feathering the length of her collarbone with his mouth before lifting his head to give her a wink. "But something tells me loud and clear, Libby McShane"—he gently grazed her lips before delving in deeper—"the fireworks are *just* beginning."

A NOTE TO MY READERS

THANK YOU SO VERY MUCH for reading Liberty and Finn's story, *For Love of Liberty*—I hope you enjoyed it! If you did, good news! You'll be able to catch up with them in my upcoming historical Western series, Silver Lining Ranch, book one of which I hope to release in the summer of 2018.

And more good news! The first chapter of book one, *Love's Silver Lining*, can be found on the next page, so I hope it whets your appetite for this fun Western series. As usual, this series will feature my signature two-tiered love story with an older Liberty and Finn along with a brand-new couple—spunky suffragette Maggie Mulaney and Finn's nephew, Blaze Donovan. Here's the jacket blurb, which not only fits for this prequel novel, but actually fits for both Liberty and Finn *and* Maggie and Blaze in *Love's Silver Lining*:

LOVE'S SILVER LINING

Book 1 in the
Silver Lining Ranch Series ...

A Match Made in Heaven?
Or Someplace a Whole Lot Warmer?

She's stubborn, educated, and
looking to give women the vote.
He's bullheaded, successful, and
looking to give her a piece of his mind.
But when things heat up, they may
just give each other a piece of their hearts.

Turn the page for your SNEAK PEEK

LOVE'S SILVER LINING

A threefold cord is not quickly broken.
—Ecclesiastes 4:9-12

CHAPTER ONE

Virginia City, Nevada, May 1885

SWEET CHORUS OF ANGELS—PINCH ME! Palms to the windowsill, twenty-two-year-old Maggie Mullaney leaned out the back window of St. Mary Louise Hospital's hallway, drinking in the heady scent of freedom and pine. For the first time since she and Aunt Liberty had fled New York—and the sham marriage arranged by her step-father—Maggie felt her ribcage expand in a sense of relief as wide and welcoming as the Sierra Nevada Mountains.

Breathing in the crisp, clean air of the mountain range that towered over Virginia City, she felt almost giddy, a sense of anticipation bubbling through her like the brook that gurgled below. *Imagine!* To practice nursing in one of the most renowned medical facilities in the country. Unleashing a contented sigh, she scanned the cloud-dappled sky with a heart of thanksgiving and a truly grateful smile. *Thank you, Lord, that I'll be serving the needs of mankind*—her smile crooked off-center—*instead of the needs of only one man!*

"Psst ... ma'am ... uh, I could sure use your help."

A gasp caught in Maggie's throat as she lurched back inside the window, almost bumping her head at the sight of a bandaged cowboy peeking out of the stairwell, gaping her jaw. And not just any cowboy.

A *near-naked* bandaged cowboy.

She swallowed hard, eyes circled in shock as she scanned from a well-worn Stetson down a sculpted torso swathed only in gauze.

A very muscular, *handsome*, near-naked bandaged cowboy.

Too stunned to avert her eyes, she was mortified to discover they had a mind of their own as they trailed past a sheet awkwardly wrapped around slim hips, the bunched material revealing muscular legs attached to mammoth bare feet. Near faint, she jerked her gaze back up to a crooked smile that literally stuttered and stopped her pulse.

Her cheeks pulsed with heat, and she immediately slapped a hand to her eyes, quite certain that none of the patients she'd treated at the Bellvue School of Nursing ever looked like the specimen before her.

"Uh, I realize this is a shock, ma'am ..." his low voice began, the barest hint of a smile lending a husky tease to his tone.

Shock? Maggie plastered another hand to her face, unable to dispel the image of brawn now branded in her brain. For the love of Florence Nightingale, this went well beyond shock to downright indecent!

"But I'd be much obliged if you'd retrieve my clothes, boots, and holster from the nurses' station, so I can go home, ma'am, avoiding scaring anymore unsuspecting young ladies such as yourself."

Maggie squeezed her eyelids shut behind her hands,

pretty sure one "unsuspecting young lady" was already scarred for life.

"Uh … miss?"

Swallowing the lump in her throat, Maggie inched a finger up to peek through her hand, mentally berating herself for allowing this man to unnerve her. For pity's sake, he was a patient and this *was* a hospital, and for the love of all that was compassionate and kind, *she* was a nurse. Or would be as soon as Sister Frederica finished her meeting with the staff and called her in for an interview.

He gave a sharp nod toward the nurses' station down the hall, and the action tumbled several sun-streaked curls onto his forehead while two deep dimples perfectly framed a little-boy grin. "Sister Fred tucked 'em under the counter for safekeeping, but as I'm sure you can understand, I'm a mite embarrassed to parade down the hall like this …" Sapphire-blue eyes held her captive, their playful twinkle all but sapping the strength from her limbs. His easy smile coaxed, joining forces with a husky whisper that seemed to slide over her like melted butter. "So if you wouldn't mind, pretty lady, I'd be forever in your debt …"

Maggie froze. *Pretty lady?* A cold chill shivered her spine while warning bells pealed wildly in her head, the sound of those two words severing the spell of the man before her faster than a physician's scalpel. The last person who had called her that had been her so-called fiancé, a society playboy with an insatiable eye for the ladies. A rogue she couldn't trust. Her eyes narrowed.

Not unlike the handsome, half-naked bandaged cowboy smiling at her right now.

With a forced square of shoulders, Maggie lifted her chin to focus only on the man's face, which was difficult enough given a perfectly chiseled jaw that sported a dangerous shadow of bristle. Quivering hands clasped at her waist, she managed a strained smile. "Why, I'll be happy to fetch your things, Mr. …."

"Donovan—Blaze Donovan, ma'am," he said with a flash of beautiful teeth that nearly buckled her at the knees. The blue eyes sheathed halfway to leisurely study her, lingering on her lips long enough to parch any moisture in her throat. "And you are …?"

"M-Maggie … uh, Mullaney," she stuttered, desperate to get this man clothed and as far away from her as he could possibly get. She struggled to project a professional air, head tipped in assessment. "I assume you are a patient, Mr. Donovan, who has yet to be discharged?"

"No, I've been discharged," he said quickly, a flare of panic in those deadly blue eyes that caused her lips to twitch in a near smile. "Sister Fred said I could go home, but she has most of the nurses in a meeting right now, so I guess they plum forgot to bring me my things."

"I see." Nodding slowly, she pivoted to make her way down the hall. "Well, I believe I saw an elderly sister at the desk, so I'll be happy to check …"

"No!"

She screeched to a stop, her suspicions confirmed. With a slow turn of her head, she peered over her shoulder, the sheepish smile he gave her downright shameless. "I mean, no need to bother her, Miss Maggie," he said with a casual shrug of massive shoulders, rugged hands pinched as white as the sheet at his waist. "So, if you'll just discreetly snatch my clothes, boots, and holster, I'll be on my way."

She spun on her heel to face him with an arch of her brow. "You haven't been discharged yet, Mr. Donovan, have you?"

"Why, of course I have, ma'am," he said with an easy drawl she'd lay good money would have gotten him far more than his clothes from every nurse on the floor. "And I'd be fully clothed and walking out of here right now if the nurses were around, you have my word." Offering an almost shy duck of his head, he cuffed the back of his neck with a bulge of a bicep that slackened her mouth, masculinity oozing out of every pore of the man's half-naked body. "So if you don't mind, ma'am, I surely would appreciate my things."

Maggie stared, in absolute awe of the raw magnetism he seemed to possess, a draw obviously detrimental to all women given the wild racing of her own pulse. Shaking off the pull, she expelled a quiet sigh, peering up with a sympathy she truly felt in her heart. "As much as I'd like to, Mr. Donovan, I'm concerned for your well-being, so I really think it's best if you wait to talk to Sister Frederica."

The roguish air vanished in the hard clamp of his jaw. "Look, lady, I've been pushed and prodded in this sick man's jail for over 48 hours now, and I'm going home whether you give me my things or not. So I'm asking you to save us both a whole lot of humiliation and just give me my dad-burned clothes."

Maggie bit hard on her lip, desperate to thwart the grin that just ached to break free. But the sight of a near-naked bandaged rogue with a tic in his temple was too good to resist, and with a sweep of her hand toward the end of the hall, she gave him a mischievous smile. "I assure you, Mr. Donovan, the humiliation will be all yours."

The blue eyes narrowed to slits of sapphire, and with a hard jerk of the sheet at his waist, he bolted past her, luring a giggle from her mouth when his bunched bedclothes whooshed by in a growl. "Thanks a lot, lady," he muttered, bare feet slapping against the wood hallway.

"Mr. Donovan, wait!" Feeling a wee bit guilty, Maggie gave chase, but the damage was already done the moment he stormed into the nurses' station. People gawked and stared in the crowded waiting room near the front door while he rifled through cabinet after cabinet, jolting a poor elderly sister out of a catnap on the counter.

"Where are my clothes?" he hissed, terrorizing the sweet old nun who darted away with far more speed than Maggie would have credited her, disappearing into the meeting room where Sister Frederica held court.

"Mr. Donovan, please!" Maggie rushed around the nurses' station, desperate to calm the man down. "You're making a scene."

He paused midway through gutting a drawer, the fire in his eyes singeing her to the spot while an entire waiting room looked on. "No, Miss Mullaney, *you're* the one who's made the scene by refusing a totally innocent request."

Her chin lashed up. "True innocence is generally fully clothed, Mr. Donovan," she said with a jut of her brow, determined that this swaddled Lothario would not pin any blame on her. "*And* possesses far more patience"—a smile tickled her lips—"not to mention clothing—than you appear to own at the moment."

Burning her with a truly scorching look, he chose to ignore her while tearing through another two cabinets, linens and medical paraphernalia flying through the air.

"Brendan Joshua Donovan—*halt!*" Everything froze mid-air except the linens when a booming voice paralyzed Maggie and every other living thing on the first floor.

He spun around to do battle like a patched-up Roman, but the sheet flaring around his straddled legs managed to steal a bit of his thunder. "Where-are-my-clothes?" he bit out, the sound as hard as the cut of his jaw.

"Safe and sound, Mr. Donovan," she said in an equally clipped tone, circling the counter with an amazing amount of grace given her wide girth. She slapped a large clipboard down on the counter to face him head-on, and Maggie stifled a grin when the sheet-clad Romeo took a step back. "Which is more than I can say for you, young man, if you don't get your carcass back to your room this instant."

He had the audacity to lean in, sheet cinched high. "Get this and get it good, Sister Fred, I am *not* going back to that cage, so unless you want me to continue making a spectacle of myself in your fine hospital here, I suggest you return my clothes to me *right now*."

Maggie pursed her lips to thwart a chuckle when Sister Frederica's intimidation ramped up with a fold of burly arms, her black habit expanding and contracting with a loud huff of air. "Don't you threaten me, young man. I wear a cornette headdress referred to as goose flaps in this town, so 'spectacles' hold no sway with me." Checking the watch pinned to her white bib, she invaded his space, the starched flaps of her white cornette headdress jerking up along with her head to sear him with a fearsome glare. Despite merely coming to his mid-chest—or mid-gauze as it were—she poked a thick finger to his chest in obvious warning. "Now I promised your uncle you would get the rest and care you need to heal properly, so if you plan on leaving my watch, Mr. Donovan, I assure you most whole-heartedly—it will be *without* your clothes."

One of the nurses tittered, and the scoundrel wasted no time in homing in on the poor girl with a perilous smile, eyes and tone softening considerably. "Do you know where my clothes are, Cassie?" he asked quietly, his tender smile assuring her she was the only woman in the room.

Honeyed curls bobbed in consent, and his smile lit up like one of those mirrored lamps used in the operating rooms of Bellvue, eyes sparkling more than the cobalt poison bottles lining its shelves. Maggie smothered a grunt. *And just as toxic, no doubt.*

"Well, then, I'd sure love to take you out for a steak dinner tonight, Cass, at the Gold Hill Hotel if you like. All I need is for you to tell me where my clothes are, darlin', and I'll even get them myself."

Maggie watched in total fascination as the girl—a petite blonde with longing in her eyes—nearly swayed on her feet, eyes locked with Donovan's as if he were a snake charmer instead of a snake. Maggie suppressed a second grunt. *A misnomer if ever there was.*

"Cassie?" he whispered, and the sound actually fluttered

Maggie's own stomach, much to her dismay, so she knew poor Cassie had to be sucked under his spell. The girl wet her lips as if she could taste the steak in question—or the man offering it—then glanced at Sister Frederica as if to plead his case.

Sister withered the tiny nurse with a scowl so potent, it eradicated every single smile in the room. "Trust me, Cassandra, I am saving you a lot of heartbreak when I say …" Thunderous brows piled low into a threat. "The bed pans on floors three and four need attending, so I suggest you begin right now."

Thwack! Maggie startled when Donovan's fist bludgeoned the counter. "That is pure, unadulterated blackmail, Sister, and you know it!"

"Not at all, Mr. Donovan," Sister said in an unwavering tone. "There is nothing 'pure' about it, much like the bribe you offered that poor girl, I might add." She jutted her chins—all three of them—in challenge.

Beads of sweat glazed the man's brow as his desperate gaze darted from face to face, the fail-proof smile appearing about to crack. "A twenty-dollar gold piece to anyone who delivers my clothes and boots," he rasped, voice hoarse with desperation, "and an evening out I promise you will never forget."

"My, what an incredibly generous offer, Mr. Donovan," Sister said with a stony smile, one thick dark brow rising in question as she surveyed her staff. "Although I doubt a twenty-dollar gold piece can provide the ongoing security of a salary, despite the pleasure of your company." Everyone flinched when she clapped her hands loudly, shooing the rest of the nurses back to their jobs. "Back to work, ladies. I assure you Mr. Donovan will soon be back in your charge."

"The devil I will," he muttered, retying the sheet around his waist with a hard jerk of the corners. "Out of my way, Sister." Shoving past the perfectly calm nun, he stomped around the counter and strode straight for the front door, still ridiculously handsome in nothing more than gauze and lumpy cotton.

"And just where do you think you're going, Mr. Donovan?" Sister Frederica demanded, bustling around the counter to keep up with the cowboy's long-legged stride. "You cannot leave here in that state of undress!"

"Watch me," he groused over his shoulder, ignoring an elderly woman who fainted dead out as he passed.

"You come back here this instant," Sister called, the boom of her voice apparently less effective the closer he got to the door. She waved a nurse over to attend to the woman on the floor. "Your dressings need changing twice daily and medication applied. And *you* need to rest."

"I don't have time to rest—I have work to do," he growled. He almost knocked a man down when he slammed through the front double doors, his sheet blowing in the wind as he barreled down the wooden steps.

The double doors banged closed, and Sister shook her head in apparent dismay, the flaps of her cornette in obvious agreement. She unleashed a noisy sigh. "A mule with second-degree burns," she muttered, turning to make her way back to Maggie who stood wide-eyed at the counter.

"Goodness, is he going to be all right?" Maggie asked, legitimate concern lacing her tone.

Sister's answering chuckle managed to escape from a mouth pursed in a tight-lipped scowl. Snatching her clipboard up, the nun made a beeline for her office, flicking impatient fingers behind her in a directive for Maggie to follow. "Well, the burns will eventually heal, Miss Mullaney, but I'm afraid the pig-headed obstinacy is here to stay." She nodded to a row of wooden chairs parked in front of her desk and then closed the door as soon as Maggie took a seat. "Nonetheless, a good dose of humility via a traipse through town in a sheet will do that boy good." She dropped into her own chair with a groan, eyes lidded with heavy folds of skin that suddenly narrowed as if weighting her down. "A mite too cocky for his own good, Miss Mullaney, and in case you haven't noticed, a wee bit too handsome for it too. Seems to think he can charm anything in a skirt, so you best be on your guard."

Blood gorged Maggie's cheeks against her will, her only defense the thrust of her chin. "I assure you, Sister Frederica, that type of man holds absolutely no appeal to me whatsoever."

The edge of Sister's lip quirked, creating a rather endearing dimple to emerge in her overly generous cheek. "And I assure *you*, Miss Mullaney, that *that* type of man can steal the affection of any female from here to Carson City. And that was *before* he risked his life to save one of Virginia City's most celebrated citizens from a fire over two days ago." She lowered her head, piercing black eyes pinning Maggie to the chair. "Liberty O'Shea's father," she emphasized, "which is why I believe you're here in the first place?"

Maggie nodded, never more grateful for Liberty O'Shea, her mother's dearest friend who had just rescued Maggie from a fate worse than death. "Yes, you see, Aunt Liberty"—she paused, feeling the need to explain—"well, she's not my aunt, of course, but I've always called her that because she's my godmother and my mother's best friend. At any rate, she asked me to come with her after she received the telegram about the fire, and since I attended Bellvue School of Nursing, I felt that St. Mary Louise Hospital might very well be the ideal place to apply for a job."

"Indeed." Sister squeaked back in her chair, meaty hands clasped over a formidable stomach. "I've already researched your credentials, Miss Mullaney, when Miss O'Shea telegrammed her request that I interview you, and her recommendation goes a long way in this town. So I'm well aware you are more than qualified from a technical standpoint." She hesitated, lips compressed so much, they seemed to disappear altogether. "My concern would be more along the emotional risks involved, given your youth and naïveté."

Maggie blinked, somewhat taken aback at Sister's remark. "I don't understand, Sister, I'm almost twenty years old— that hardly qualifies as either young or naive."

"Perhaps not in New York, Miss Mullaney, but this is Virginia City, where there are over one hundred saloons, give or take a few, within a very small radius. That's one drinking establishment for every thirty-two people, my dear, which means a lot of what we see in this hospital has to do with a very rowdy and very lascivious male component." She lifted in her chair ever so slightly to assess Maggie's House of Worth coral silk dress, from its voluminous skirts to its tightly fitted bodice. Her gaze instantly flicked up to Maggie's chestnut hair, which she'd jumbled on top of her head in a cluster of ringlets and a frizzle of soft bangs. A weary sigh escaped her lips. Sagging back in her chair, she studied Maggie through slatted eyes that held a trace of a twinkle. "I don't suppose you'd be willing to wear a sack?"

Relief coursed through Maggie's veins, assuring her she would do whatever it took to acquire this position. "Absolutely," she said without hesitation, "I would be more than willing to wear whatever you like, Sister, including a gunny sack."

Sister's mouth curled into a dry smile. "Over your head?"

Maggie stilled, all blood ceasing to flow until she realized Sister Frederica was joking. Her face flushed so hot, she was certain she resembled a saloon girl with rouge on her cheeks. *Wonderful. I should fit right in.*

Sister hovered over her desk with a squeak of her chair, hands clasped and dark brows knit low as she bent to meet Maggie eye to eye. "Frankly, Miss Mullaney, I'm a wee bit worried you can't handle the element here. Suppose you tell me why I should hire an innocent like you, merely to expose you to one of the most sinful cities in this nation?"

With everything in her, Maggie strove to remain calm

despite the awful hammering in her chest, knowing full well the fate of her future lay in this woman's hands. Silently drawing in a deep swell of air, she met Sister's gaze head-on, a slow smile wending it's way across her lips at the memory of a near-naked cowboy decorated in cotton and gauze. She arched a brow. "Because the arranged engagement from which I fled, Sister, was to a man like your bandaged cowboy and any other womanizer just like him. Rest assured I have no interest in men like that or really any men at all." She sat straight up in the chair, shoulders back and lips firm, unflinching as she locked gazes with a woman she'd come to respect in mere minutes. "In fact, I find myself greatly inspired by women like Florence Nightingale and you, Sister, wondering if perhaps my calling isn't to remain single altogether, forgoing on the servitude of marriage so that I may serve others instead."

A smile twitched at the corners of Sister's mouth. "Which I assure you will be more than a challenge in a city where the number of men far exceed the number of women, my dear." She paused, her eyes narrowing in scrutiny. "Then may I assume that our 'near-naked cowboy' had no affect on you whatsoever?"

Some of Maggie's bravado faltered a bit when blood coursed into her cheeks, but she ignored it with an unyielding lift of her chin. "I won't lie to you, Sister. Mr. Donovan does have a certain"—she swallowed hard—"charm, I suppose, but I quickly proved to myself and to him that I am immune."

"And how exactly did you do that, young lady?" Sister asked, forehead in a squint.

Maggie nibbled at the edge of her smile, the memory warming her eyes to a twinkle. "Well, you see, he was hiding in the stairwell at the end of the hall when I went to look out the window, and the poor man tried every tactic in the book to coerce me into retrieving his clothes." She lifted a hand, ticking off Mr. Donovan's methods in a sing-song manner. "Flirting, teasing, begging, guilt, seduction ..."

"Pardon me?" Sister jutted a brow.

Her smile took a twist. "He flexed a bicep," she explained with a dusting of heat in her cheeks, adamant that no cowboy—half naked or otherwise—would ever get past her defenses.

The nun's low throaty chuckle surprised her, and the satisfied grin on Sister's face immediately unraveled any knots Maggie may have had in her stomach. "Well, well, young lady, you just may be exactly what I'm looking for then, as long as you can steer clear of heartbreakers like our Mr. Donovan. But it won't be easy."

"And why is that?" Maggie wanted to know. Yes, no doubt the rogue was one of the finest looking examples of manhood Maggie had ever seen, but it would take a whole lot more than a chiseled face and body to turn her head.

"Because, my dear, Brendan Donovan is not only handsome and charming to a fault, but he is also the foreman for his uncle's Silver Lining Ranch as well, which he has helped parlay into the largest, most profitable ranch in all of Nevada."

Wonderful. A hardworking example of manhood on top of handsome and charming. Maggie gulped. *But it still wasn't enough.*

"And then, of course," Sister continued, an unmistakable look of affection flickering across the old nun's face, "he's utterly devoted to his family, a veritable hawk when it comes to watching over his two little sisters. Not to mention a staunch mentor for his younger brother who works in a bar, much to his uncle's disdain."

One side of Maggie's mouth tipped up. "His mentor? In drinking and womanizing, no doubt?"

Sister sighed. "Regrettably, you're correct about the womanizing, but the man has never touched a drop of alcohol as far as I know. Which is why he's so dangerous to the young ladies of Virginia City. Especially since he scaled a burning staircase to save little Frannie after rescuing both Liberty's mother and housekeeper, who were asleep in their rooms."

"No!" Maggie could do nothing but gape, absently wondering if a cowboy could be canonized. "Please tell me the child wasn't hurt!"

Sister's mouth took a tilt. "A ferret, actually, and no, Maeve's beloved pet came through unscathed, which is more than I can say for Mr. Donovan. The poor man incurred several nasty nips from the ferret in addition to second-degree burns." The twitch at the edge of Sister's lips hinted at humor. "A female ferret, of course, lending credence to the saying, 'Hell hath no fury like a woman scorned.'" She gave Maggie a wink. "Or in this case, a ferret mourned."

Maggie couldn't help it—she grinned.

Sister sighed. "No, there's no question about it. Brendan Donovan is a hero with a heart of gold," Sister continued with a shake of her head, "but with more stubbornness in his veins than silver in the Comstock." She bent in, her smile dry. "And trust me—they don't call him 'Blaze' for nothing, my dear. He has a reputation for setting hearts on fire, and as the town's confirmed bachelor, I'm afraid he leaves a lot of charred ruins in his wake."

Sister lumbered to her feet and extended a hand, which Maggie instantly took, the nun's warm and welcoming palm flooding her with a sense of safety and peace. "Which means, young lady, I am going to take a chance on you if you can steer clear of Mr. Donovan and any rogues just like him, understood?"

"Oh, yes, ma'am," Maggie breathed, hardly able to believe she had landed her very first job!

"Good." Sister toddled around the desk and gave Maggie's arm an affectionate squeeze. "You start on Monday, Miss Mullaney, and your job will be to put those impressive skills to work on behalf of our wounded. And *my* job, my dear," she said with an outrageous wink that took Maggie completely by surprise, "is to keep *you* from being one."

ABOUT THE AUTHOR

JULIE LESSMAN IS AN AWARD-WINNING author whose tagline of "Passion With a Purpose" underscores her intense passion for both God and romance. A lover of all things Irish, she enjoys writing close-knit Irish family sagas that evolve into 3-D love stories: the hero, the heroine, and the God that brings them together. Author of The Daughters of Boston, Winds of Change, and Heart of San Francisco series, Julie Lessman was named American Christian Fiction Writers 2009 Debut Author of the Year and has garnered 18 Romance Writers of America and other awards. Voted #1 Romance Author of the year in *Family Fiction* magazine's 2012 and 2011 Readers Choice Awards, Julie was also named on *Booklist's* 2010 Top 10 Inspirational Fiction and Borders Best Fiction list.

Julie's first contemporary novel, *Isle of Hope,* was voted on *Family Fiction* magazine's "Top Fifteen Novels of 2015" list, and her historical novel, *Surprised by Love,* appeared on *Family Fiction* magazine's list of "Top Ten Novels of 2014." Her independent novel *A Light in the Window* is an International Digital Awards winner, a 2013 Readers' Crown Award winner, and a 2013 Book Buyers Best Award winner. Julie has also written a self-help workbook for writers entitled *Romance-ology 101: Writing Romantic Tension for the Sweet and Inspirational Markets.* You can contact Julie through her website and read excerpts from each of her books at **www.julielessman.com.**

OTHER BOOKS BY JULIE LESSMAN

FOLLOWING ARE JULIE'S NOVELS, NOVELLAS, and a writer's workbook. All are available in both e-book and paperback except for the novellas, which are available in e-book only.

The Daughters of Boston Series
Book 1: *A Passion Most Pure*
Book 2: *A Passion Redeemed*
Book 3: *A Passion Denied*

The Winds of Change Series
Book 1: *A Hope Undaunted*
Book 2: *A Heart Revealed*
Book 3: *A Love Surrendered*

Prequel to The Daughters of Boston and Winds of Change Series
A Light in the Window: An Irish Love Story

O'Connor Christmas Novellas
A Whisper of Hope
(formerly part of *Hope for the Holidays* anthology)

The Best Gift of All
(formerly part of *Home for Christmas* anthology)

The Heart of San Francisco Series
Book 1: *Love at Any Cost*
Book 2: *Dare to Love Again*
Book 3: *Surprised by Love*
Blake McClare Novella: *Grace Like Rain*
(formerly part of *With This Kiss* anthology)

Isle of Hope Series
Prequel Novella (*FREE DOWNLOAD!*): *A Glimmer of Hope*
Book 1: *Isle of Hope—Unfailing Love*
Book 2: *Love Everlasting*
Book 3: *His Steadfast Love*

Silver Lining Ranch Series
Prequel Novel: *For Love of Liberty*
Book 1: *Love's Silver Lining*
Book 2: *Love's Silver Bullet*
(Coming in 2019)

Other Novellas
The Gift of Grace (formerly part of *Cowboy Christmas Homecoming* anthology)

Romance-ology 101 Writer's Workbook
Romance-ology 101: Writing Romantic Tension for the Inspirational and Sweet Markets

Made in the USA
Monee, IL
28 May 2024

59021560R00121